Fake Biker __ , ___

BEARS OF FOREST HEIGHTS BOOK 3

Roxie Ray

© 2021

Disclaimer

Table of Contents

Prologue - Sting

It was really nice to not play lookout anymore. I would have done anything for Hutch, but it was a relief that things were finally getting back to normal. The little rescue operation had been a month ago and my life was back into a more or less normal rhythm. It was crazy how chaotic the club had been lately. First Rainer getting kidnapped and us storming the Chaos crew compound, then Kim getting kidnapped. Like, what the hell? At least we weren't bored, I guessed.

I was at the bar working, and it was my last night. My last night ever slinging drinks for someone else. For the past year, I'd been squirreling money away, working on a secret project. I enjoyed working at the bar, but I'd always wanted my own place. Not a dive like this, but an upscale place. I didn't look like it but I enjoyed the finer things in life. Caviar? Champagne? Foie Gras? All right up my alley. Don't get me wrong, I'd keg stand with the best, but there was something rewarding about living life to the fullest.

I bought a building right downtown, and over the last few months, I'd been having it renovated into a lounge. Everything was running right on time and the grand opening was in about a month. I had a bunch of social media pages and posts lined up, and ads in every paper within an hour's drive. There was a pack meet in a couple of days and I planned on announcing my endeavor to the whole crew. I couldn't wait to see Hutch's face. Even he didn't know about all of this.

I walked behind the bar and started prepping my stuff for the night. It was early on a Friday, but it was already packed. A bunch of regulars knew it was my last night and it looked like they all came out for a parting word. I hoped they would all come out to my new place when they found out.

I ducked out for a quick bathroom break before things really got crazy. I got halfway there when I picked up the beginnings of an argument between a man and woman with my sensitive ears. It *was* the weekend so I wasn't surprised, but I also did double duty as security here. I slowed down to try and see if it was going to escalate.

"I said I have a boyfriend." the woman said.

The guy replied hotly. "Well shit, baby, I'm not gonna tell him if you don't."

I sighed and rolled my eyes. It was typical shit. It would settle down on its own, and I turned to continue to the bathroom.

But then I heard her yell. "Don't fucking touch me."

I stopped in my tracks. I hated aggressive assholes. What part of the word *no* was so difficult to comprehend? I turned to push through the crowd toward them.

"I said I have a boyfriend." Her voice sounded a bit more panicked and a lot angrier.

"Well, he's not here, is he? Someone needs to keep that fine ass company." I heard the sound of a palm slapping an ass, and I walked faster, gritting my teeth.

Damsels in distress were my weakness. I didn't have a hero complex like some guys, but I couldn't stand seeing women being put in situations like this by assholes like that.

I broke through the crowd and saw the altercation. The guy looked half drunk already. The girl turned toward him, yelling. She had an amazing body, but it didn't give this guy the right to force her to do anything. I slipped behind her and wrapped my arm around her waist.

"Hey babe, sorry I'm late. You good?" I asked.

She turned to me surprised. I had my own moment of surprise. She was one of the girls who'd been at the bar with Kim all those weeks ago. I recovered and gave a look that said *play along.* She took the bait and leaned into me.

The douchebag looked me up and down, and seeing my shifter mark he glanced at her and snarled. "Are you fucking serious?"

She wrapped her arms around me, and shockwaves went through me. She was fucking gorgeous, and I was like a thirteen-year-old boy hugging the prom queen. Barely, I was still able to play my part.

I looked at him but spoke to her. "Who's this fucking bozo? And why does it seem like he's bothering my girl?"

She laid her head on my chest. "Just some guy who can't take a hint. Tony, we've been over for a *long* time. And don't forget you ended it. And...you've moved on. Right? Aren't you about to marry—"

She got cut off as another woman, who looked mysteriously like the girl leaning against me, came sliding up and wrapped an arm around Tony. I sighed. The story was starting to come clear.

"Hey babe, there you are. Couldn't find you." she glanced over at us and looked at me, surprised.

"Alexis, who's this?" the new girl asked.

Tony piped up. "It's *apparently* her new boyfriend."

The girl looked at Alexis and sighed. "Ugh, seriously? Why didn't you tell me? If you were going to be a plus one for the wedding, I needed to know."

The girl with me, *Alexis,* opened her mouth to respond but the new chick cut her off.

"Of course you'd do something like this right before your own sister's wedding."

Yep, I read this right. Of all the holy audacity. The sister then asked, "Are you her plus one for the wedding? If so, I need to know so the planner can get things moved around."

Alexis grew stiff beneath my arm, tightening her grip on me. I reached out to shake the sister's hand.

"My name's Sting."

She put her hand forward. "I'm Bridget, and this is my fiance Tony. I can't tell you how glad I am that Alexis is *finally* moving on." She blew out a breath and rolled her eyes.

Behind Bridget, Tony looked anything but glad. He stared daggers at me over Bridget's shoulder. I looked back at him and grinned and winked.

"Can't wait to see you guys at the wedding," I said, still playing my part.

Bridget took Tony by the arm and led him away. "Nice to meet you." she called back as they left.

Alexis sagged with relief as they disappeared. Turning to me she smiled gratefully. "Thanks. You have no idea how much I appreciate it. I'm sorry you got dragged into my family drama. I'll make some excuse about why you won't be at the wedding."

I looked at her, and...fuck she was beautiful. I didn't want to call the whole game off. For whatever reason, I wanted to play the damned thing out.

"Nah," I said.

Alexis frowned. "What?"

I shrugged and grinned. "I don't like making plans and breaking them without reason."

She narrowed her eyes at me. "Well, that's too bad. These are some plans you'll have to break."

I looked up at the ceiling and pretended to think it over. "Nope. Can't think of anything I'd rather do."

Alexis tried to argue, but I put my hand up walking away. "I gotta get back to work. You'll hear from me soon though."

Alexis called across the floor. "You don't even have my number."

"Oh, I have ways of finding things out." I turned away and walked back to the bar. I was smiling when I got there. Just when life was getting back to normal...

Chapter 1 - Alexis

The morning sun felt amazing on my face. It helped me forget about last night. How awkward and irritating the whole thing had been. Tony had been his usual asshole self. The nerve of him acting like that with Bridget right there in the club. What the hell was he thinking? He hadn't been thinking, not at all. He was still hung up on me, and I didn't know if he'd ever get over that. It was going to make family holidays super weird every year.

Putting on a pot of coffee, I leaned against the counter and thought about the guy who'd stepped in the night before. Sting? What kind of freaking name was that anyway? Sounded like a stage name. Was he a musician? Wrestler? Porn Star? Who the hell knew. If not for him, though, things might have gotten even more ridiculous. He totally saved me some embarrassment with Tony and Bridget.

I couldn't let him go through with the charade of being my boyfriend, though, even for one night at the wedding. I needed to end it before it all went too far. He seemed like a nice guy, and he didn't deserve to get pulled into my family drama for no good reason.

After I poured a cup of coffee, I grabbed my phone, ready to put a stop to this. Unlocking the phone I realized I didn't have the guy's number and set it back down. He said *he'd* find *me*. Shit. How the hell was I going to get in touch with him? I needed to do it soon. It was Sunday, and I had brunch planned with my family. I did *not* want to endure that painful disaster, while also worrying about this fake boyfriend.

My cup was almost to my lips when my cell started ringing. Glancing down I saw it was an unknown number. Something tickled at the back of my mind. Intuition maybe?

"No fucking way," I whispered, picking the phone up.

I hit the green button and squeaked.

"Hello?" I cleared my throat. "Hello?"

"Told you I had ways of finding things out," Sting said.

Sighing, I chuckled. He was resourceful. "Okay, I'm not even going to ask, I'm just thankful for your timing. I need to see you this morning. I've got brunch with my family in like an hour and a half. Can we meet up?"

"Sure thing." Well, wasn't he bright and bushy-tailed this morning? "You know where the shifter compound is outside town?"

Nodding to myself, as if he could see me, I said, "Yeah, of course, I do."

"Well, okay then. See you in like twenty minutes. Unless you drive like a granny, then I'll see you in thirty."

I snorted. "Twenty it is." I hung up and rushed to finish getting ready. I wanted to get this over with and head straight to brunch, then get *that* over with.

Less than five minutes later, I pulled out of my driveway and headed toward the outskirts of town. I'd heard Kim talk about the place, but in all my time in Forest Heights, I'd never been to the compound. It kind of had a weird allure to it. Debauchery, fantasy, danger, fun. The whole shebang. Though, about fifteen minutes later, I found myself a little disappointed with the reality of it. I hadn't been expecting a biker-slash-shifter amusement park or anything, but the random scattering of buildings and gravel parking tucked into the woods was a little anticlimactic.

Before I could walk up to the main building, a door opened off to the side, and Sting stepped out into the morning light.

"Well well well, if it isn't my beautiful new fake girlfriend."

He looked different in the daylight. In the club the night before, he'd seemed like a cute, charming guy. With the sunlight shining on his dirty blonde hair and that scar across his eyebrow? He seemed far more intimidating—still gorgeous though. I pushed that out of my head. It wasn't why I was here. I was here to get things settled.

"Okay, listen, we need to figure out a way to keep you from going to the wedding," I said, cutting to the chase. "A plausible excuse. Any bright ideas?"

His smile never left his face. "Why would I want to do that? Are they getting somebody gross to cater?"

Great. The guy was as funny as his name. Not very. "Jesus, come on. There's going to be so many questions we won't be able to answer. How did we meet? What do you do for a living? How long have we been together? My whole family will figure out really quick that this is all a sham. Then *I'll* look like a total idiot."

Sting raised his hands like he was warding off an attack. "Whoa, now. That's a pretty easy fix. We'll just come up with something. We can hammer out all those questions in an afternoon. Then we're good to go. Right?"

Shaking my head I said, "It's more trouble than it's worth." I sighed and looked up at the sky. "I'll tell my sister we broke up or something."

"Or." he exclaimed, holding up a finger. "You bring me and make your ex jealous."

I stared at him for several beats before I said, "How did you know?"

He smiled again. "I read the room. It wasn't hard to figure out. Honestly, and I'm not trying to be a dick, but do you really want to watch your ex marry your sister all by yourself?"

My cheeks flushed with embarrassment. Most of the town knew. I wasn't stupid. I realized it was all over the place, but that didn't stop me from hating it. Living in a small town like this, it was par for the course. Irritation filled me. I'd grown tired of going back and forth with Sting.

I turned and walked back to my car, yelling over my shoulder. "You aren't coming. That's final."

Before he could respond, I slid into my seat and slammed the door. Doing my best to not slam the gas and spray gravel all over him, I pulled out of the parking area. It wasn't his fault, but shit I was irritated with the whole thing. He'd made things worse. And now I had to go have eggs damn benedict with the whole King family.

I pulled up at my parents' house a few minutes later. They owned a gargantuan house in a gated community, and I hated it. I grew up there, but it was enormous and over the top; not my style at all. I preferred things to be a little subdued, less in-your-face. If I'd ever said that out loud though, my mom or sister would probably look at me like I said I wanted to bathe in whale vomit or something equally disgusting. I sat in my car for several minutes, working up the courage to go inside.

Ugh. Tony's Porsche was here. I'd known he'd be here, but I'd been hoping for a miracle. When I'd waited as long as I could, I got out of the car and went inside.

Brunch was as awkward as I'd thought it would be. Mom had told us she'd made a full spread. Scrambled eggs, waffles and toppings, bacon, sourdough toast, potato hash, a salad with herb vinaigrette, and most randomly, crab cakes. It looked like she was trying to feed an entire basketball team instead of five people. And by her saying she *made* everything, it really meant she watched over the maid and private chef as *they* prepared all the food.

The beginning of the meal was fine, but it was awkward seeing Tony snuggled up against Bridget. It was really hard to not remember all the times I'd sat with him like that. It made me a little sick to my stomach watching them, but I played my part of the happy sister. I didn't like seeing him with my sister, but I definitely didn't want to see him with me again.

Tony's eyes were on me, off and on, through the entire meal. I wiped my mouth with a napkin and looked up. He wasn't even concealing it at this point. It made me almost unbearably uncomfortable. I slid my eyes over to Bridget.

She'd noticed Tony watching me. Instead of punching him in the side or calling him out on his creep behavior, she decided to turn on the bitch switch and go after me.

Bridget put her fork down, interlaced her fingers, rested her chin on them, and looked at me with that sugary sweet look she got right before she did or said something shitty.

"Alexis, aren't you going to tell Mom and Dad about your new thug boyfriend we met at the bar last night?"

I bit the inside of my cheek and smiled back at her, trying to come up with a retort.

Mom looked up with wide eyes. "Alexis? A boyfriend?"

I tilted my head, annoyed. "Don't sound so surprised, Mom. And he's not my *boy*friend, he's just a *friend.*"

Bridget didn't let up. Glee flashed in her eyes when she said, "That's not what she said last night. They looked all cozy. Oh." She covered her mouth like she was surprised by what she was about to say. "*And* he's a shifter."

Mom dropped her fork and gasped. "A shifter? Alexis, we raised you better than to associate with people like that. Barely better than animals..."

She went on and on, berating me, but I tuned her out and glanced back over at Bridget. She beamed, as she watched me get a verbal lashing. Tony seemed not to notice anything as he stuffed half a crab cake in his mouth. I bit down on my tongue again, trying not to scream at them or at my mom.

My Dad seemed to have finally had enough, thank goodness. "Darina. Stop it. Alexis is free to date whomever she pleases."

Mom's shoulders slumped, and she looked at Dad like he'd lost his mind. "Sam, what will people think?"

He looked at Mom pointedly. "Darina, me being a black man, people would have said the same thing about you dating me if we'd grown up in the fifties or sixties. Is that the kind of person you want to be?"

Mom looked cowed, but not as much as she probably should have.

Dad went on. "Not all shifters are bad. Our daughter has admirable character, and I'm sure she wouldn't choose anyone that wasn't good for or *to* her." Dad's eyes locked onto Tony and my ex wilted visibly under the glare.

Bridget looked pissed. Her little game hadn't gone the way she'd wanted. She wouldn't question our Dad, though. Especially since it was Dad who was writing all the checks for her over-the-top wedding.

Ugh. I was ready to be anywhere from here and set my napkin down. "This was fun and all, but I need to go. Oh, and Bridget, don't worry, Sting won't be coming to the wedding."

Under her breath Mom mumbled. "Sting? Really?"

I continued ignoring her. "He won't mess up your picture perfect wedding pictures."

Bridget looked pretty smug when I said that, but Dad broke in. "Now wait a minute. You need to bring this boy to the wedding."

I gaped at him. So, did Bridget, who opened her mouth to protest. "But Daddy—"

He held up a hand to shut her up. I had to bite my lip again to keep from laughing.

He looked at me and said, "You should be able to bring whoever you want. And if this man wants to accompany you, then you should let him."

I stared at him for a few seconds, not really sure what to say. I was torn. On one hand, I wanted to be done with the whole charade, but on the other, flaunting something in front of Bridget on her big day was seriously tempting. It was juvenile, but damn it, it was true.

I nodded. "Okay, Dad. I'll think about it."

Bridget glared at me as I said my goodbyes and made my way out the front door. I sat in my car for a few minutes, letting myself recover. That wasn't enough, though. I needed to vent, so I started my car and dialed Kim.

It rang twice before she answered. "Hey, girl. What's up?"

I sighed and started in on an extended rundown of the night before and the disastrous morning while I drove aimlessly around. By the time I finished, Kim was almost crying, she was laughing so hard. Hearing her horse laughs made it all seem a bit better.

"Okay, okay. Enough humor; what should I do?" I smiled to myself.

Kim composed herself and said, "Honestly if it was me? I'd take Sting out of spite. Make Tony the dick look like shit. But even if not for that reason, Sting is actually a really cool guy. He'd be great company if you want someone to hang with who can get your mind off of that disaster of a

wedding."

I told her I'd think about it and said goodbye

before driving around for a few more minutes.

Eventually I gave it up, sighed, onto the highway

heading back toward the compound to see Sting

for the second time that day.

Chapter 2 - Sting

I was getting excited clicking the right arrow on my laptop, flicking through the images of the chairs I'd bought for the lounge. They were the very last purchase that had to be made and I'd gone over and over *and over* it for days before finally pulling the trigger. They would be here a couple of days before we opened. It was nerve wracking and anxiety inducing but still exciting. It was almost time to open. My dream was about to come true.

"Yo. Sting. Got a visitor." Rogue called from the front door.

I frowned and glanced up to see Alexis standing outside. What the hell was she doing back? I wasn't mad, not at all, just confused. I set my laptop aside and stood, smiling at her as I walked over. "Hey. Funny seeing you again so soon," I said, "What can I do for you this time?"

Alexis chewed at her lip, looking extremely annoyed. It was adorable. Alexis seemed like one of those girls who were perpetually miffed. She finally sighed and shrugged, flopping her hands at her sides. "Okay so, I know what I said before, but you are going to be taking me to the wedding, if you're still willing."

I stared at her for a beat before laughing. "Well what in the hell changed over the last three hours? Was it my devilish good looks?" I turned in a circle, feigning looking at my butt. "This tight ass? What?" I teased.

She grinned, but it was forced. She was hiding her frustration. She was good at hiding it, like me, but I saw through her. I knew that feeling all too well; trying to cover up all the negative emotions inside. It gave me an inkling that we had a connection, a shared habit. But also, since I totally understood, I stopped pushing.

"Sorry, just joking. Of course, I'll take you. But, for real, why the change?" I asked.

Alexis visibly relaxed after I agreed, like a huge weight lifted off of her. "I'm sorry, too. This whole back and forth thing? I'm sure you have other things in your life that need attention. But thanks. I would tell you all about my fucked up family life but I'll spare you the details." She hesitated. "Well shit, I guess if you're taking me you'll see for yourself. I'll let that be a surprise."

I chuckled. "Okay, cool. Though, like you said this morning, if we're gonna pull this off we need to get to know each other. I mean, if we are supposed to be dating, I should know some basic stuff. Right?"

She stared at me for several seconds, her hazel eyes boring into me. A rush went through me, seeing her gaze locked on me like that. I couldn't explain it, even to myself. It gave me an intense tightness in my chest, like a tug that couldn't be ignored. I pushed it away and decided to fill the silence.

"So, uh, what does your schedule look like for the next few days?" I asked, quickly adding. "If we're gonna pull off the whole couple thing, it might be good to be seen together right? Small town and all?"

She ducked her eyes away nervously and nodded. "Yeah, sure. You're right. I'll text you my work schedule and all the wedding stuff. Pictures, rehearsal dinner, ceremony, all of that. We can figure out some times to hang out, be seen, get our story straight?"

I let a slow smile spread across my face. This was going to be a lot of fun. "Sounds like a plan to me."

Alexis sighed and gave me a pointed look. "I'm warning you, it's a lot. Like...a *lot*." She drew out the last word dramatically, and I had to laugh.

She finished. "If you're gonna back out, now's the time, big guy."

I crossed my arms and gave her my best smile. "I'm always up for a challenge."

She sighed again and smiled. "Okay, don't say I didn't warn you though."

With that, Alexis turned and walked back to her car. I tried not to watch her walk away, but...well, the view was too good. I waved as she pulled away and I glanced at my watch. The electricians were supposed to be at the lounge installing the final lights. I decided to head down and see how everything looked.

A twenty minute bike ride later, and I was walking into my place. It looked freaking great. I was getting more excited by the minute. The grand opening was only one week away, and each day I had to remind myself this was real. I stood watching the installers for a few minutes, my hands on my hips like some captain watching his crew hoist the sails when my phone rang.

It was my mom. She called me daily, without fail, to check in. Even though I went to visit a couple of days each week, the calls came like clockwork. "Hey, Mom."

"How's my baby doing?" she asked.

I rolled my eyes and smiled. "I'm fine, just down here checking on a few finishing touches on the lounge."

"Oh, that's right. You're only a few days out aren't you?"

I nodded. "Yup, one week and it's show time. The lights are getting hung today, my first alcohol shipment is in two days, and I just ordered the chairs. They'll be here in three or four. It's all coming together."

"Reese, I am so proud of you. I really am. I'm trying to talk myself into coming, but it might be a little crazy for someone my age."

My Mom was the *only* person who used my real name, and it made me grin. I had no doubt she wanted to be here for the opening, even though she lived about an hour away. She'd gotten a place of her own about ten years ago, once she hit menopause. As difficult as that life change was, it was one of the things female shifters had to look forward to. Once it happened, they were no longer physically able to shift, and they were no longer deemed a *threat to society* and could live anywhere they wanted. They didn't have to be relegated to the outskirt compounds that all other shifters had to live in.

"Come if you can, but it'll be a late night, so I'll understand if you can't get here," I said.

I wanted to show her what I'd built, but she was more of a homebody. Fingers crossed, opening night *would* indeed be crazy. She might find it too exhausting.

It always made me happy when my mom said I made her proud. That was the one thing I'd always strived for from the time I was a very small child. I wanted to honor my mother. Mostly to make up for what my dad had put us through.

Almost like she'd read my mind, Mom said, "So, I need to tell you that your father called again."

My mood soured instantly, and I gripped the phone tight in anger. Just hearing *about* him was enough to drive me into a rage. I hadn't seen the man since I was nine years old. He'd walked out on us, leaving Mom and me with nothing. We'd had to move away from all my family and friends, and come to Forest Heights to live with my aunt. I tamped the anger down and tried to keep my voice calm. "Well, that's nice. I still have no desire to see the scum bag. I don't want to talk to him or even hear about him. Honestly Mom, I wish you'd block his number," I said.

Mom sighed and said, "He's changed, Reese. He's a different person now."

Shaking my head and looking up at the ceiling in frustration, I tried to keep my fury stamped down. I couldn't answer yet.

"Really honey, it would be healthy to just speak with him and get some stuff off your chest."

Needing to get off the call as quickly as possible I said, "Oh, shit, Mom, there's a plumber here. I need to show him something. I gotta go, I'll come to see you soon. Love you, bye."

I stuffed my phone back in my pocket and stood there feeling like shit for lying to get her off the phone, but damn it, I did *not* want to talk about that jackass. I stewed for several minutes there, getting angrier by the minute. I needed to get out of here before I started banging and hitting shit and scaring the electricians and contractors.

A few minutes later, my bike screamed down the road. I pushed it a little faster than I would usually have been comfortable with, but the wind helped calm me down. Once back home, I slammed the kickstand down. Anger still pulsed through me, and I needed to relieve some tension. Running into the yard behind the clubhouse I shifted. My body formed into the bear, immediately I felt better, though it didn't last long.

Trees shot past me as my paws slammed into the ground, my claws digging in as I pushed myself faster and faster. Trying to run away from all the memories of my dad. The only memories I *had* of him were bad. All the times he'd screamed at me and at Mom. The way his hand felt as it slapped me across the face. It all bubbled up, all the emotions I kept bottled up in human form. They were stronger and more virulent as my bear. I couldn't stop what came next.

Sliding to a stop, I huffed and slapped the ground with my paws, rage still building. Finally, I sat back on my haunches and lifted my muzzle to the sky to let out a roar. It went on so long even my bear throat was raw by the time I was done. Hanging my head, I turned and walked back through the woods, toward the compound. The shift had only made me feel worse, more miserable, which was depressing. Shifting was usually one of the things I always counted on to raise my spirits.

I shifted back to human form before stepping out of the trees, lifted my head, and came to an abrupt stop. Grizz stood there in the backyard looking at me. He had his hands on his hips, his massive shoulders creating an imposing figure. He didn't seem upset. In fact, he looked worried.

"Sting? You all good?" he asked.

Nodding reluctantly, I shrugged. "Yeah, fine."

Grizz looked at me and raised an eyebrow, obviously not falling for my shit. He said, "I heard you out there. It's what brought me outside. That roar sounded heartbroken. I wanted to check on whoever made it."

Heat crept into my cheeks as they reddened. I hated looking weak. It was terrible and embarrassing. It was even more terrible and embarrassing to do it in front of the Alpha of the pack.

Though, if I assumed Grizz would hold it against me, I was wrong. Grizz stepped forward and put an arm around my shoulders. "Come on bro. Let me get you a drink. It looks like you need it," Grizz said.

He led me back into the clubhouse and into the back where a long bar was built into the common room. Grizz stepped behind the bar and grabbed a few bottles off the shelf.

"Okay, what'll you have? Sex on the Beach? Fuzzy Navel? Harvey Wallbanger?"

I snorted despite myself, and shook my head. "How about Jack and Coke?"

Grizz bowed his head once and laughed "Glad you said that. If you'd asked for a pussy drink I'd have to rethink your membership."

We sat in silence for a few minutes, each of us sipping our drinks. It was easy to see that Grizz wanted to know what was going on with me, but to his credit, he didn't push.

Finally, Grizz said, "Sting, you know you can tell me anything right? I'm the Alpha of this pack, and it's my job to take care of everyone. It's also my job to make sure everyone is taken care *of*. Now those two things may sound the same, but I assure you they are very different. No matter what's going on, the pack is here. You aren't alone."

I nodded and chewed at my lip as I finished my drink, trying to think of how to respond. It made me feel good, knowing the pack and Grizz had my back no matter what. Even so, I was not in the mood to talk. Especially not about my dad. But there was something I could talk to Grizz about. I needed advice.

I looked up. "This is not really what I'm upset about, but I do need your perspective on something."

Grizz chuckled. "Perspective? Aren't we a little mister fancy pants all of a sudden."

I grimaced and waved him off. "Yeah, yeah. Anyway," I said, emphasizing the word. "I met Kim's friend Alexis last night at the bar. Her ex was being a dick and whatnot. I stepped in and pretended to be her boyfriend to get rid of him." I paused. The story was already getting convoluted and confusing. "Well, long story short, her ex is marrying her *sister*, and I'm taking her to the wedding. When I was talking to this girl, Alexis, today, there was this weird tug in my chest. It was like I was being pulled toward her. I've never felt anything like it before. Have you ever experienced something like that?"

Grizz laughed and downed the rest of his own drink. He put the glass on the counter and stared at it for several seconds.

When it looked like he wasn't going to say anything, he looked at me and said, "Sting, my man, you've always been a little impulsive. And that story proves it. Pretty ballsy stepping up into the fake boyfriend role right?"

Grimacing, I nodded and stayed quiet.

Grizz smiled ruefully. He had a look on his face I couldn't quite decipher, and said, "Not sure how this will play out friend, but go in with an open mind and you might be surprised."

I didn't think about what he'd said for long. Just as he finished talking my phone buzzed. Grabbing it I saw it was Alexis texting me. She'd sent her schedule for the week. I smiled and mentally began planning our first 'date.'

Chapter 3 - Alexis

Sting finally responded to my text from the day before. He'd sent me an address and said to meet him there when I was done with work. It was cryptic and vague to say the least, but whatever. I tried not to dwell on everything too much while I worked.

Kim and I got all the kids packed up and out the door to their parents by three. All that left was the cleanup.

Kim looked at me and said, "I'll do all this. You have a hot date to get ready for."

I immediately stood and threw a stuffed monkey at her. "Fake date. Fake, damn it."

Kim laughed at me and knocked the toy out of the air before it got to her. "Weren't you the one looking for a—What was the term you used? You wanted to *find a little biker boy of my own*, isn't that what you said?"

I pressed my lips together and huffed a breath out my nose. "Now, that was said because I was trying to get you laid. It wasn't really for my benefit," I lied.

Kim made a shooing motion with her hands. "Sure, right. Now get the hell out of here. Your biker boy won't wait forever."

I didn't dignify that with a response. I grabbed my backpack and purse and went out the door. It was a nice day out, the late summer sun kept things warm and delightful. If the wedding had not been on the horizon, taking up every bit of my extra brain space, I could have really enjoyed the weather. I sighed, got into my car and called the address back up that Sting had sent. Pulling out of the lot I asked myself for about the millionth time what in the actual hell I was doing.

The GPS took me to an area near downtown. The building looked a little sketchy. Sitting in my car, I looked around. There didn't seem to be anyone else here. I chewed at my fingernail, trying not to go down the rabbit hole of negative thoughts. Was I getting screwed with? Was this a

gang thing? Jesus...was Sting gonna rob me or

something?

Finally, I shook my head. No, the outside of

the place looked really nice. It wasn't some sleazy

motel or decrepit warehouse. The front door

stood wide open, and I decided to go ahead and

look inside. Sting was probably in there

doing...something. I locked my door and walked

across the parking lot and through the door, then I

stopped dead in my tracks.

"Oh, wow." I whispered to myself.

This place was cool as hell. It looked like the

nicest upscale club I'd ever been in. The large

room was dark, but not dreary. Lots of whites,

blacks, and silvers decorating the club. A nice bar stretched across the back of the room, glass shelves behind it for alcohol, and a large area in the middle with tables. I turned in a slow circle looking at everything, a bemused smile on my lips.

Sting's voice echoed from the back. "Well, how do you like the place?"

Spinning around, I found him smiling and leaning against another, smaller bar. His dirty blonde hair hung loose around his shoulders. I decided, right then, that if I was going to have a fake boyfriend, at least I had a hot one.

"This place is amazing. Is this where you work? Who owns this place, and why have I never heard about it?" I asked as I walked toward him.

He grinned even wider. "Well, the reason you've never heard of it is because it's not open yet. Grand opening is on Friday night. I hope to see you there. To answer your other two questions..." He held up fingers as he answered. "Yes I do work here, and the reason I work here is that I own the place."

If he owned the place, what was he doing working as a bartender? This guy was a jokester. He was messing with me. Frowning, I said, "No, for real. Who's place is this?"

Before he could answer, a guy appeared from the back with a cardboard case. "Hey, boss. The wine glasses came in. You want me to start polishing and setting them behind the bar?"

Sting nodded. "Sounds good, Luke. Thanks."

My eyes widened. He was telling the truth? He owned this place? My face grew warm as I realized what an ass I'd made of myself.

I put a hand on Sting's arm. "Hey, I'm sorry. I didn't mean to sound like I didn't think you could own the place."

He smiled, completely unfazed. "I don't really look the type, do I?"

I sighed. "I guess I'm more like my mom than I want to admit. She's the type to judge a book *and* the author by its cover. I should know better. I mean." I laughed and swept an arm around the club. "Why can't a biker-bear-shifter-bartender own a classy joint, right?"

Sting didn't seem offended. Instead, he took me by the arm and gave me a tour. He showed me the bar up close, then the dining area, the dance floor, the kitchen, even the bathrooms—which were the nicest I'd ever seen. They had freaking bidets for frick's sake. He walked me back over to the bar when the tour was over, and we took a couple leather clad stools.

Sting said, "So, for our first." He held up quotation fingers. "*Date,* I wanted you to come help taste test the menu. We can come up with our origin story while we eat. Are you game?"

I realized I'd barely eaten anything at my parents' house before my awkward departure. I was starving. Laughing, I nodded eagerly. "Sure. But we need the story to be good, but believable."

A few minutes later, a guy in a black chef's coat came out of the kitchen carrying two platters, setting them before us. Sting patted him on the shoulder as the chef departed. Glancing down, I didn't really recognize anything on either platter. My tastes weren't as elevated as the rest of my family.

This looked fancy. Sting could probably see the confusion on my face.

He pointed at each item as he named them. "Chicken croquette with white wine mustard sauce, crab and corn fritter, heirloom eggplant and burrata roll, scallop sashimi lettuce cup, gorgonzola and bacon stuffed quail legs, and caviar on a cornmeal crisp with creme fraiche and minced egg. Dessert will be out later."

I looked back at him with my brows furrowed. "I don't even know half the words you just said."

Sting laughed again; he seemed to do that easily. I actually liked him a lot, which would make this whole debacle a lot less painfully awkward.

He said, "Trust me, it's all good. Let's get to the story. I want something dramatic. Like maybe you were getting mugged, and I rescued you. Something like that, if we're doing this."

Rolling my eyes I said, "My parents won't believe something like that. Wouldn't it make more sense that we met through Kim? Like, isn't that how almost *every* relationship starts? Friend of a friend? Simple, but sweet."

Sting gave me a look that told me he wanted a juicier story but would go along with mine. "Okay, fine. Try some of the food."

I picked up the chicken thing and popped it in my mouth. I bit down and literally moaned in pleasure. "Oh, my gosh, that's good. It's like—"

"The best chicken nugget you've had in your life?" He finished for me.

I nodded. "Holy crap."

His smile widened, and he took a bite for himself. We tried everything—twice—while we came up with the story that we'd met a few months back and that Kim had introduced us. We'd hit it off immediately.

"Because I was so sexy?" Sting asked, biting into the caviar.

I rolled my eyes again. I'd done it several times in response to his corny jokes. "Anyway... We kept it quiet until we knew we were serious about each other. Once we were sure, we couldn't stay away from each other. Almost love at first sight or something."

It really was a sweet story. It gave me a pang of sadness. I wished it was a true story instead of a made up lie. Not necessarily with Sting, though. It had just been so long since I'd had *any* romance in my life. Dating app swipes were not my idea of a romantic life.

I went to grab another bite of food and was dismayed to see we'd finished everything. Sting saw the pouty face I made and chuckled. He stacked the platters neatly aside and grabbed me a beer from the cooler behind the bar. "Well, we can come up with some other questions at our next date. Sound good to you?"

A little nagging worry started at the back of my mind when he said that. I needed to set some stipulations and boundaries to make sure Sting knew this all make believe and not the start of something real.

I put my hands on the bar. "Okay, some ground rules."

Sting took a swig of his beer. "Oh shit, here it comes."

I ignored him and continued. "We are playing a part, but it doesn't need to be crazy. Displays of affection should be at a minimum. Hand holding? Sure. Kissing? Light pecks on the cheek or lips, no tongue."

He slapped the bar dramatically. "Oh, come on, Mom. You are no fun."

Ignoring his antics, I continued laying down the law. "And if you're pretending to be my boyfriend that means no banging other chicks until the show is over. I can't have my family seeing you grabbing some other woman's ass when you and I are supposed to be all lovey-dovey."

Sting set his beer down. "Okay. I accept the terms. Consider me celebate until the vows are said." He held out one hand. "Let me walk you to your car?"

I nodded, and as we walked out, I glanced around at the lounge once more, getting excited to come back Friday and see it in full swing.

Sting put a hand lightly on my back as we walked across the parking lot. It was nice. Warm, comforting. How odd to feel this way.

I was digging in my purse for keys when his hand stiffened. Glancing up at him, I saw him looking at me and smiling, but something was off.

Barely moving his lips he whispered, "Play along." He pulled me to him. "Wrap your arms around me."

I did as he said, and he leaned down toward me like he was going to kiss me. Instead of pressing his lips to mine he put his face against my neck and whispered to me. "We're being watched."

My body stiffened, wondering what the hell he was talking about.

Sting continued. "Woman in a red BMW. Parking lot of the gas station across the street, giant sunglasses."

My eyes swiveled over, but I already knew what I would see. I groaned and gritted my teeth. "It's my fucking mother."

He sighed in relief. "Is this normal behavior?"

I shook my head. "No, but after my sister told my parents about our supposed relationship, Mom is worried about the *family image*."

His grip relaxed, but he continued holding me, standing erect and looking down at me. Right then, for an instant, the barest second really, a flush of desire for him ran through my body. A flash of imagination that left a cinder of heat in my belly...and *maybe* a little lower. I shook my head quickly, brushing the tingling away.

Sting leaned down and gave me a peck on the cheek, like we'd discussed. "Get home safe okay?"

I nodded and forced myself not to glance over at Mom spying on us. I got in the car and waved to Sting as I pulled away. At home, a few minutes later, I plopped down on the sofa.

I couldn't stop thinking about the *date*. It was all fake, one hundred percent, but even then, I'd enjoyed my time with Sting. He was a really cool guy. And apparently very driven, looking at the work he'd put in on his club.

I picked up a book I'd been working on reading and tried to lose myself in it. I really needed to not think too much into the thing with Sting. I'd worked for years to keep my feelings locked away. It was way easier to do that than to get hurt again. Hurt the way Tony hurt me. Being closed off was lonely, but heartbreak was far worse.

Unable to focus on the book, I made myself a quick salad and sandwich for dinner and went to bed early. Laying down, trying to sleep, my thoughts rolled again to Sting. I remembered how strong and thickly muscled his body had been when I'd been pressed against him. How charming and funny he was. It was a story, a fabrication, and he was doing it for my benefit, but what if it wasn't just a story? What if it was real?

Chapter 4 - Sting

We were a couple days away from opening, and my nerves were starting to get frayed. The little tasting date with Alexis the other day had been a nice distraction, but now the full weight of what I was about to undertake was setting in. It was exciting, but the closer the opening came, the more my nerves distracted me. I had a lot of grand ideas too: this was only step one. There were other business ideas bouncing around my head, but this was the first and most important.

Until we opened officially, I'd installed a generic door chime to let me know when vendors or workers came and went. The sound of the chime broke me out of my nervous mental gymnastics.

I didn't have any deliveries scheduled for today. It must have been someone looking around, trying to scope the place out. I stood up from my desk in the back office and made my way to the front to let them know we weren't open yet.

But instead, I stopped dead in my tracks when I saw who it was. It wasn't easy, but I tried not to smile like an asshole seeing Tony Givens standing in the middle of my club.

I affected my best customer service voice. "How can I help you sir?"

Tony stepped toward me, his face all stoney and pissed off looking. He was a big dude, and had played professional football for a short stint. I'd looked him up.

I was still bigger, *and* I was a shifter. He was trying to intimidate the wrong fucking guy right now. It wasn't going to work. I asked again. "Sir, what brings you to my fine establishment? How can I help?"

Before answering, Tony glanced around, checking the place out. "Nice little joint you got here. Looks like it cost a pretty penny, am I right?"

I smiled. "It was a pretty big investment, yeah."

"Hmph, all I can wonder is." He looked me up and down. "How could someone like you come up with that kind of cash? Quick money usually isn't honest money. You know what I mean?"

I smiled at the insinuation. He was fishing for information. No way I was giving this schmuck the satisfaction of getting me pissed.

I shrugged. "I invested well, saved, and worked hard. This is the payback for all of that." I let my jovial attitude slip away and become serious. "Now, do I really need to ask you again why you're here?"

I wasn't at all surprised when Tony got his hackles up and pointed at me. "You and Alexis need to be done. Got it, big guy? You are not even close to being in her league." His upper lip curled. "Some biker? A *shifter* biker at that? Probably grew up in some fucking trailer on a filthy ass shifter compound didn't you? Christ, you don't even realize how little you fit into the life we live. She's too good for you, bro. Figure it out and get out of her life."

I gave him a wry smile and tilted my head. "Tony, *bro*, you don't really have any place to talk do you? What with you marrying Alexis's sister?"

He threw out his arms, growing more agitated. "Hey, man, you don't know shit about shit. Don't talk about what you don't understand."

In contrast to big Tony, I was cool as a cucumber. "No, I know all about you, big guy. High school hero, a big jock getting any scholarship he wanted. Drafted to the big leagues, but jacked up your leg before you could get any traction there. Came back home with your pride all hurt, so you started slamming your dick into your ex-girlfriend's sister. Shit not only that, but now you're gonna *marry* the chick?"

Tony's face turned scarlet red, his rage like a bomb ready to go off. The only thing keeping him in check was the fact that he knew I was a shifter.

I kept going, enjoying it. "You probably don't really love her, or even want to marry her. You got pushed into it by the family. Yours? Hers? Doesn't really matter. You did it, despite the fact that you knew it would tear Alexis apart. Also, while you're balls deep in the sister, you've still got a thing for Alexis..." Oh, his face was purple now. "Probably only broke up with her because you thought you were going big time. The big league. Thought you'd be the next Tom Brady. Thought you'd have a centerfold, a bikini model, maybe even a famous actress sucking your cock by now." I held up one finger while he sputtered. "Except, here you are, back in Forest Heights, and the grave you dug is too deep to crawl out of. It just pisses you right the fuck off because you can't have her back." I smiled at the rage on his face. "How'd I do?"

Tony's anger finally got the better of him, and he took a step toward me, balling up his fist.

I raised an eyebrow. "Think twice, *bro*. You're aren't ready for that kind of trouble."

Tony stopped moving, frozen by my words, and I realized he may not have been entirely as stupid as he seemed.

He pointed at me again. "You still aren't good enough for her."

That may or may not have been true. "Well then it looks like we're in the same boat, huh?"

Without another word Tony spun on his heel and stormed out. Before he was out the door I had my cell out and was dialing Rogue.

"Yo." Rogue answered on the third ring.

I cut to the chase. "Hey, I got a real douchebag cramping my style. And this dude somehow figured out where the lounge is, and the fact that

I'm the one that owns it. Anyway you can find out

how he dug all that up?"

"Uh, maybe. Do you at least have a name?"

"Tony Givens."

He paused. "Wait like, *the* Tony Givens? The

football star from back in the day?"

Ugh. *The* Tony douchebag. "Yeah, yeah, the

guy that washed out of the league."

"Okay, at least he should be easy to track

down. I'll dig into his stuff and see what I can find.

I'll go whole hog, phone records, credit card

transactions. Do you want me to see if he's

searched for any beastiality porn or anything?"

Way too far. "Gross, dude. Nah. Just the basics, I just want to know how he found me."

"Cool, brotha. I'll get back with you when I'm done."

"Thanks." I hung up.

I tried to go about my day after that, but I couldn't get my mind off of it. I didn't like how Tony acted so comfortable, rolling up on me like that. Dude had to have balls of steel to walk onto a shifter's property and try to warn him off of a woman.

After about an hour of trying to focus on spreadsheets for the lounge, I gave up and decided Alexis needed to know her ex was being nosy about her love life. I sent her a text asking her to come to the lounge.

She agreed and came walking through the door a little less than an hour later, looking pretty happy to see me, which was nice. I wanted to be on her good side; she was a cool girl.

"What's up?" she asked as she leaned on the bar.

I sighed. "Well, there's no easy way to say this. You're gonna be pissed though." I proceeded to tell her about the entire altercation with Tony. By the time I was done I could almost see the steam coming out of her ears.

"That mother fucker. He comes in here?" Alexis threw her arms up and stormed away from the bar. "And says *you* aren't good enough for

me?" She stomped back toward me. "After all

the..." She sputtered. "Absolute *shit* he's put me

through?"

I didn't speak, just nodded, letting her get it

out.

She nearly snarled, which honestly was

incredibly cute. Not that I'd ever say that in this

moment. I had no death wishes. "I wished you'd

beaten his ass right here."

I laughed.

"Can't have a bar fight before the place even

opens. Anyway, I don't want to pry, but what

really went down with you two? I made some

assumptions to piss him off, but I'd like to know

the whole story. I mean, we are dating, you've probably already told me."

Alexis snorted and rubbed at her temples. "Yeah, sure."

I pushed out a bar stool with my foot. "Cool, have a seat. Let me get you a drink. What do you want? Martini?"

"Shot of vodka."

I stopped and looked at her. "Just...a straight shot?"

She slapped the bar. "Hell, yes. I need it. Only one though. I've got to drive home."

"What the lady wants, the lady gets." I poured her a shot and walked it over with a beer for myself.

Alexis slammed the shot and winced before starting. "So, Tony and I were high school sweethearts. Disgustingly cliche, I know. We were together from about the middle of sophomore year on. He got a big time scholarship, so I decided to go to the same school to be close to each other. Got an apartment together. Honestly, I really thought we'd get married. He played well, won a bunch of trophies, and then he got drafted after junior year. I was excited for him, like, stupid excited." She sighed and tossed back her empty shot glass, looking for any leftovers. "Then, the *night* of the draft mind you, he dumped me. Said his agent told him he needed to focus on football and didn't need any distractions. Said he couldn't worry about women when he wanted to win a championship."

Geez. The dude really was a douche.

She continued. "After that, I finished my degree and tried to drown my heartache with school work. I graduated and headed back home, to move back in with my mom and Dad." Dark laughter burst from her lips. "Then I had to suffer the indignity of watching the only guy I ever loved on TV all the time. He started the first three years, and I saw him at awards shows and galas with these young little starlets all over him. Ugh, so stupid."

A small smile transformed her face. It was a petty grin, but still cute. "He played like shit though. He couldn't translate his skills to the pro game. That made me feel a little better." She laughed. "He bounced around the league for a few years as a backup. Then about two years ago, he shredded his knee. During practice no less. I guess something went wrong with the surgery and rehab. He basically couldn't play anymore, and he washed out. He came back home and kind of disappeared for a while."

I broke in. "That dude laid low? He acts like he's King Shit of Turd Mountain. How could he stand not being the center of attention?"

Alexis laughed. "You've got him pegged. He eventually showed up at my parents' house. I'd believed he was there to...I don't know. Apologize for what he did to me? Grovel for me to take him back. But, imagine my surprise when I realized he wasn't there for me, but for my sister."

I couldn't believe what I was hearing. "Hold the hell up. How fucked up is your sister to do something like that to you? Like really? She'd start banging your ex?"

Alexis shrugged. "I'm used to it. Bridget always took stuff from me. I think she got off on it. Toys when we were little, clothes when we were older. But I didn't really anticipate my ex-boyfriend being one of the things she would scoop up for her own."

I wanted to hug her but held back. "Alexis, you are so much better off without that douche."

She straightened up. "Oh, don't I know it. Don't get me wrong. I'm not still pining over Tony. If he threw himself at me right now, I would first vomit, then tell him to get lost." She looked at me, suddenly apprehensive. "Sting, are you sure you still want to go through with this? I don't want to make trouble for you. Not with your place about to open."

I shook my head. "After what you just told me? And what that dick said earlier? I'm even more fired up than before to pull this off."

She smiled, and I smiled back, taking a drink of beer. It tasted as sweet as wine right then.

Chapter 5 - Alexis

Friday night came pretty fast. Sting and I decided over text that the big grand opening of his lounge would be the best time to debut our relationship.

Sting had ramped up the social media and advertising the last three or four days, and everyone in town was talking about the opening.

He'd been trying to keep it under wraps that the place was owned by a shifter, and it sounded like the place would be packed.

Even the other teachers at the school I worked at were talking about going and checking it out.

Everyone in town would be there. At this point, I was worried that Tony and Bridget would show their hateful selves up.

If nothing else they'd want to see if it turned into a disaster so they could gloat about it. Even if they did, I had no doubt the club would be a resounding success.

It made me happy for him, but it also made me extremely nervous. I hadn't been out with a man in over a year. The prospect was too exhausting after all the failed dates and jackasses I'd tried dating since Tony.

In fact, I was so anxious that I'd had to pull Kim aside the day before and vent. She'd done a good job of calming me down, and had promised that she and Hutch were going to be going

anyway to support Sting. She said she would be

there for my benefit too.

Almost like clockwork, my phone buzzed

with a text from Kim saying she was outside to

pick me up. I checked my mascara and lipstick one

more time, grabbed my small clutch and was out

the door before I talked myself out of it. Kim

looked amazing as I slid into her passenger seat.

"You ready?" she asked.

I shrugged. "Still nervous. It's just...I don't

know. Such a big lie."

Kim laughed. "But worth it. You can shove

all that crap back into your Mom and sister's faces

at the wedding. You'll be walking in with the

hottest guy in the room, bar none. And you'll look happy, and that *will* piss off Tony. Like, it's a win-win."

"You're right, but still, kind of nerve wracking."

We talked about random things for the next ten minutes until we pulled up at the lounge. My jaw fell open.

Beside me Kim whispered, "Well, damn."

Guys wearing red jackets took keys in front of a valet station, smiling and parking cars. Spotlights shined and music blared.

The line to get in was *huge* and wrapped around the side of the building. It literally looked like some Hollywood premier or the Oscars or something. We pulled up to the front door and a valet opened our doors and took the car away, leaving Kim with a ticket. A couple dozen motorcycles were parked across the street, not surprising. I doubted any of Sting's crew would let someone else park their bikes. They must have all been inside already.

Kim took me by the arm, and we walked up to the line and saw the velvet rope, like honest to goodness velvet, keeping the line organized. I turned to walk to the rear of the line, but Kim tugged at me. She nodded to the door. One of the two bouncers at the door seemed to be looking at us and beckoning us with two fingers.

Walking toward him, I asked Kim. "Does he know who we are?"

Kim nodded. "Remember. You're supposed to be Sting's girl. Do you really think he wouldn't have his doormen looking for you? The club owner's lady does *not* wait in line."

I giggled at the thought and started forward, only to be stopped by my sister. Lovely. She tossed her hair over her shoulder and glared at me. "Where are you going?" Bridget asked, her gaze darting between me and the bouncer.

Kim stepped forward. "Her boyfriend owns the place. She was silly for standing in line in the first place."

Bridget gaped at me, then stuck her nose in the air. "I didn't realize what sort of dive this would be, if he owns it." She glanced at her friend, who looked about as fake and snobby as my darling sis, and jerked her head. "Let's go. We can't be seen here with these people."

I stepped back and smiled. "Perfect," I whispered to Kim. "Now I won't have to worry about running into her again all night."

Kim giggled and grabbed my hand and the Bouncer escorted us past the head of the line and into the club. The music was loud, but not obnoxious. It was the right volume to make the club feel exciting, but let conversations happen. People milled everywhere; it really was packed.

The bouncer led us to a private table in the corner. Glancing around the room, It was obvious that everyone was having a great time: people dancing, drinks flowing, food coming out of the kitchen. I smiled despite myself.

Before we could even get settled, a server sat what looked like sparkling water in front of Kim and a glass of champagne down in front of me.

"Courtesy of the proprietor. Enjoy," she said with a smile, then disappeared back into the crowd.

Kim laughed and picked up the glass. I grabbed mine, and we toasted before taking a sip. Looking around again, I felt a strange sense of pride. I had to remind myself that it wasn't my

real boyfriend who owned this palace, but damn it

was impressive. I also already considered Sting a

friend, and it was fine to be proud of a friend's

accomplishment.

We relaxed for several minutes and enjoyed

the vibe of the place until the server returned

with menus. I saw several items I'd tried the other

day, along with many more I hadn't. I ordered a

few things to try. Hutch and Grizz stopped by our

table for a few minutes to chat before heading

back into the crowd. The whole night was like a

dream, a very good dream.

About an hour later, after we finished

eating, the music turned down and a spotlight lit a

small stage at the far end of the lounge. Sting stood beneath the light, and I raised my eyebrows and my jaw fell open again.

He held a microphone in one hand and champagne in the other, wearing a fitted tuxedo that showed off his athletic body with his hair pulled back into a tight ponytail, and his beard and mustache freshly trimmed. He looked like some bad boy movie star from the forties. Dangerous, classy, clean, and *gorgeous*.

Beside me, Kim put her fingers in her mouth and released a piercing wolf whistle, which made Sting laugh.

He chuckled into the mic then raised it closer to his lips and started speaking. "I want to thank everyone for coming out on our first night. It really means so much to me. Many of you are friends and family, but most are here to see what the whole big deal is. Hopefully we are meeting your expectations." The crowd clapped and cheered for several seconds before he continued. "When you have a dream, I say you have to pursue it. I hope everyone who is here tonight is chasing a dream. Chasing it and hopefully getting close to grabbing it. There is nothing on this earth like doing the thing you love. And I have to say, it looks like all my dreams are coming true." He raised his glass and tipped his head toward me. The entire crowd turned to look at me, and my face grew hot. The spot light also swung around to illuminate me, to my intense mortification. "I want everyone here to have a great night. Enjoy yourselves, drink, and be merry. I'm going to go say hello to my lady."

My stomach clenched. A few hoots from the crowd accompanied Sting as he handed off his mic and stepped off the stage, walking straight toward me, still under the spotlight. I stared at him, my eyes wide and shocked, and if I was totally honest with myself, a little starstruck. He stopped at the table, striking an imposing figure, before leaning down to me, cupping my cheek and giving me a gentle and sweet kiss on the lips. A flush of heat went through my whole body as he pulled away. I was a little disappointed that he didn't continue the kiss. Then I remembered the strict rules I'd given him about PDA. I chastised myself for that little decree. Too late though.

Sting said, "You look amazing."

"So, do you. I didn't think a biker could dress so well," I teased, regaining some of my composure.

He looked at himself and chuckled. "I guess I do clean up pretty good."

He slid into the booth with us and chatted for a while. Several of the members of the crew came by to congratulate him and to tell him how great the place was. None of them were dressed as nice as Sting, but most of them did an admirable job of cleaning up. It was really great to see how much support he had from them. Every single one of them seemed truly happy for Sting. Many times I'd noticed my father's business associates and friends congratulate him, but it always seemed like there was an undercurrent of jealousy in it. Here it seemed to be true family-like love. It made me happy to see, and I understood how Kim had been able to fall into this group of scary biker bear-men.

I wondered how much support I would get from my family if I ventured out to do something as grand as what Sting had done here. Sadly, I couldn't see it happening. My sister would make a joke of it, Mom would tell me I needed to settle down and find a husband. Dad would probably just be terrified I'd fail and be unhappy.

Those thoughts put me into a foul mood, but I pushed them away so I didn't ruin Sting's big night. I shook it off and turned back to the conversation. I was surprised to see Sting looking at me, concern on his face. He'd been paying more attention to me than I'd realized.

He touched my hand. "Are you okay? You look upset."

"I'm good. It's fine." I smiled up at him gratefully. He really was sweet.

He leaned close and pressed his forehead against mine. "Something made you upset, it's written all over your face. If it's something I can fix then tell me, and I'll fix it."

His words shot butterflies all in my stomach, and my heart skipped a beat. It was nice to have someone care if something had upset me, even if I was a little confused by his concern. Nobody was close enough to hear us. Was he putting on a show to make the relationship seem more convincing? That's probably what it was. It was nice to pretend though.

I forced my best fake smile. "No for real, I'm fine. There's nothing to fix."

He stared into my eyes for a few seconds. He looked like he wanted to say something, but his gaze broke away when someone called his name.

He turned back, grinning. "Okay I need to make the rounds and mingle. I'll be back to get you guys another order. Whatever you want, it's on the house."

He gave me a quick kiss on the lips and floated into the crowd. I stared after him for a few seconds, then turned and finished my drink. Kim looked at me over the rim of her soda and lime.

"Are you sure this is pretend?" she asked.

Glaring at my best friend, I tried to formulate a response as the butterflies in my stomach danced the Mamba. "Oh, it's definitely pretend," I said. The words sounded weird even to me. But I couldn't afford to catch feelings for this guy, so it was pretend. It had to be.

Kim shook her head and smiled. "Didn't look fake to me a minute ago."

I sighed and ran a hand through my hair. "Don't think too much into it. He's putting on a show. He's a good actor, but that's the extent of it."

Kim put a hand on my arm. "Yeah, well what if he isn't acting? Huh?"

I looked up, letting myself think about it for a couple seconds, watching the dancing lights on the ceiling.

I finally let out a breath, shook my head, and said, "Don't put those ideas in my head, that's not a thing that's gonna happen."

For most people, that would be enough to drop it, but Kim being Kim, she continued pushing the idea.

"Why can't it? Give me one reason."

I was getting frustrated, but I didn't have a good answer for her. Did I think I didn't deserve happiness? Was it fear of a relationship? Or maybe fear of rejection? Who knew? After all the disasters I'd been through, I didn't see it ever happening for me.

Kim must've seen I was upset. She took my hand. "Hey, I get it. I really do. Maybe you should open your mind to the possibility that this little pretend show could turn into something real for both you guys."

I knew that I was smart, and pretty, and a good catch, but it seemed that every man I'd ever been with had shit all over me and my heart. I wasn't keen to start something new. I did sneak a glance back out to the dance floor and saw Sting shaking hands and laughing with a group of customers. He did seem like a really good guy. Maybe, if I left the door cracked a little, something might come of it.

I finally looked at Kim and said, "I'll think about it. But that's all."

I didn't see much more of Sting, him being busy trying to work the crowd. We hung out for another hour, and had several more drinks. I was pretty tipsy when my bladder decided it was time for a little break. I got up and worked my way through the crowd to the back alcove where the bathrooms were. Before I even got to the doors I spotted Sting and another woman. My heart pounded watching her move her hands all over him and nuzzle at his neck. I frowned and turned around, fighting tears as I walked straight back to the table. Sting called my name, but I ignored him and didn't stop.

I stepped up to the table and tapped my knuckle on it to get Kim's attention. "I'm ready to go. I'll be outside."

Kim looked surprised and confused. "What happened? You look pissed."

"Don't want to talk about it, I just want to go."

"Uh...okay, sure. It's getting late anyway."

I walked out the front door before Sting could find me, and waited for Kim. I stood there getting more and more pissed off at myself for even allowing myself to imagine Sting might truly want me.

Why would *anyone* want me? I bit the tears off before they could fall, and spent the car ride home pretending to be asleep so I didn't have to talk about it. My phone vibrated from calls and texts, but I ignored it. I didn't want to interact

with anyone or anything.

Plus, I really had to pee.

Chapter 6 - Sting

Shawna was a regular at the compound parties, and she'd always had a thing for me. We'd hooked up quite a few times, but that was the extent of it. I wasn't surprised she was here, but I *was* surprised she was pestering the shit out of me. She kept searching me out. The only time I'd been able to get rid of her for any amount of time was when I'd sat with Alexis and Kim. I was at the bar talking with the cocktail manager when a hand slid up my back.

I turned and saw her there, and couldn't help but sigh. "Shawna, sweetie, I'm working. I can't spend my whole night talking to you. Okay?"

She was pretty lit and had the half lidded look of someone who'd had about three drinks too many. "I just want to know about this little girlfriend you've got. Why is she so fucking special, huh?"

I sighed, and decided the best way to get away from her this time was to take a leak.

"Shawna, I need to piss okay. Go find a nice young stud and see how much fun you can have."

Without another word, I escaped to the bathroom. I did piss, but I also just leaned against the wall after washing my hands. I was pretty tired after the lead up to opening and all the adrenaline from tonight. I just needed a few minutes to recharge. A few splashes of water on my face and a couple of minutes of deep breaths, and I stepped out of the men's room. I only got three feet before she found me.

"Sting, seriously. What does she have that I don't?"

Jesus Christ, she was like a dog with bone. She had me cornered and pressed herself up against me. She slid her hands across my chest and looked up at me sweetly.

"I used to make you feel good. Didn't I? Does she do the things I did? If she does something good, I can learn new tricks."

I would never hurt a woman, not after what I'd watched my dad do to my mom. The thought didn't even register. I put my hand on her waist to gently push her off, but she shifted her hips so my fingers slid down her butt. I pulled my hand away and tried to move her away from my chest, but she pressed forward and put her face right in my throat and kissed my neck.

Enough. I was already getting pissed, but then the smell hit me.

Alexis.

Her scent, and it was close. My gaze jolted up and scanned the crowd. I spotted her, walking away from us. There was no way she didn't see this little scene, and even though I was trying to get Shawna off me, it couldn't have looked good. *Fucking shit.* "Alexis."

She kept walking. I tried to move around Shawna to go after her, but she tripped over her own feet and started falling. I stretched out a hand to catch and steady her. She grabbed my lapels and pulled me close, still trying to kiss me. That was enough, god damn it.

I pushed her gently against the wall so she could steady herself and released her. "Leave me the fuck alone. I'm done. Got it?"

Before she could answer, I turned and made my way through the crowd. I pushed through until I made it back to the table Alexis had been, but she was gone. I glanced up and saw Kim open the front door and Alexis standing out on the sidewalk. I rushed toward them, doing my best to politely move around customers. I had to stop once and shake someone's hand, it took all I had not to scream at him to let me get out the door.

When I was finally able to get to the parking lot, a valet was closing the door of Kim's car, and they drove away.

"Ah shit." I said, pulling my phone out of my pocket.

I dialed Alexis's number and listened as it rang seven times and went to voicemail. I then sent her a text basically saying it wasn't what she thought it was. I stood there staring at my phone for nearly fifteen minutes waiting for the little *read* symbol to appear beside the message. When it became apparent that she wasn't going to even open the message, much less respond, I went back inside.

Grabbing one of the guys I had working security, I pointed out Shawna.

"That girl? Get her the fuck out of here. I don't care what her tab is, I'll pay it myself. Get her gone, and blacklist her. I don't want to see her face in here again. Got it?"

He nodded. "You got it boss."

The rest of the night was a huge success. I only wished I'd been able to enjoy it. I was in a pissy mood all evening, though I didn't let it show.

I still put a smile on. I shook hands, mingled, and did all the things an owner needed to do.

Last call was at one-thirty, and we had the final guest out by a few minutes after two in the morning. I took off the tux in my office and put on a t-shirt, shorts, and sneakers. Then, I helped the crew shut down and clean up everything.

I was in my own bed before four. I hoped to get six hours of sleep before I had to wake up and do it all over again.

I'd hired a manager for the place, so it wouldn't be an every night kind of thing. It seemed like the right thing to do as the owner, at first at least. I needed my face to be seen constantly on the opening weekend. I drifted off to sleep wondering what Alexis was thinking.

The next morning, the first thing I did was try to get a hold of Alexis. After the fourth call that went to voicemail and the sixth text that went unread, I threw my phone on the couch. It was driving me crazy that I couldn't even get a moment to tell her what had really gone down the night before. I bounced around my place for a bit before the nervous energy got me out on my bike. I wound my way through town and eventually ended up back at the clubhouse.

I barged in and slammed the door behind me, still pissed. The only other person there, randomly, was Trey. He sat on the couch reading a book. At the slammed door, he glanced up calmly and raised an eyebrow. "What's gotten into your undies?"

I sighed and flopped down on the couch beside him. Not sure what to say I blurted. "I fucked up. Well...pretty sure I did anyway."

Trey put his book down and stared at me. After a few seconds he said, "This is where you tell me what the fuck you're talking about."

I smiled despite myself, and went on to explain what had happened the previous night. I didn't go into huge detail about the fake part of the relationship, just the fuck up parts.

I concluded. "I understand why she's pissed off, really I do. I just wish she would let me explain. Even if she cussed me up and down afterward and told me to get lost, it would be better than this. Just waiting."

Trey leaned back, and by the look on his face, he was thinking it over . It was weird how much he'd changed the last year or so; it was almost like a whole new person in Trey's body.

Finally he asked, "What's her dating history like?"

I looked at him, confused. "What do you mean?"

Trey bobbed his head back and forth and said, "Like, has she had a history of being with guys who..." He paused and chewed his lip. "Maybe they've let her down? Cheated? Or chosen other women over her? Stuff like that? Could be why she acted put off that quickly."

My mind flew to Tony, and the shit he'd done to Alexis. I fell back on the couch, realization dawning on me. Damn it.

I put my hands to my face. "Shit...Fucking shit."

"Bullseye?" Trey asked.

I dropped my hands and nodded. "Pretty much. I stepped in it. Maybe I can figure a way out of the mess I made. We'll see."

We sat for a few minutes in silence before Trey said, "Hey Sting? Can I ask you a question?"

Trey sounded nervous, something else I'd never heard in his voice.

"Yeah bro, what's up?"

He placed his book to the side and said, "Do you need any help at the lounge? I'm home for good now, and I need something to keep myself occupied. I wondered if you might have something I could do to help out. At the club, I mean."

I smiled and put a hand on the back of his neck. "Bro. For you? I'd find a spot for you any day."

It made me happy that he asked me. Talking to Hutch and Grizz and seeing with my own eyes, it had been a hard road for Trey. He'd worked his ass off to get his shit together. It made me feel good to help him out. "Come by Monday when the place is empty, around eleven or noon. I'll be there then. We can talk about it."

Trey clapped his hands together once in excitement. "Thanks, man. That would be awesome."

The rest of the day seemed to grind by with me checking my phone every ten minutes to see if Alexis had read or responded to my messages. She hadn't.

After what seemed like days, although it had only been twenty-four hours, I ended up at the lounge, dressed in a fresh tuxedo, ready for night number two. My mood did pick up a bit just before the doors opened, after I checked the social media pages for my new place. Nearly every review was great.

The building was packed within minutes of opening. I was thrilled with the response, and I made my way through the crowd thanking everyone for coming, having drinks with a few different folks. I even bought a round of drinks for a group of ladies who were there having a bachelorette party. Even with all of that, I couldn't get my mind off of Alexis. I decided that if I wasn't able to get a hold of her directly, I would go the next best route.

Ducking into the kitchen and out the back door I pulled my phone out and dialed Kim.

It rang twice before she answered. "Hey asshole." She sounded irritated but not enraged, so that was something.

I winced. "Hey. Has Alexis talked to you?"

"Uh...yeah. Took me all of last night and most of the morning today to finally get the story out of her. Why are you such a dick, Sting?"

"Wait. No. Listen, please." I proceeded to tell her what actually had gone down and why it looked so bad.

There was a long pause before she replied. "Well shit. She's pissed either way. Like, one of the only rules she gave you was to not whore yourself out while you were pretending to date. And you were doing it right there in public?"

"But I said I wasn't—"

"Yes, I know. That isn't what she saw though, Sting. It makes the whole plan look dumb."

Irritation flashed over me. I was a little pissed that Alexis was only mad because the show we were putting on might get ruined. It was stupid for me to be upset. There'd been a couple little moments, a look here or there where it didn't quite feel like it was pretend. At least for me, the moments felt that way.

"Okay, fine. I know, okay? Can you at least pass along what really happened? Ask her if she can call me or stop by the lounge? So, I can talk to her in person."

"Sure, I'll talk to her. Not sure what it might do, but I'll put a bug in her ear."

I told her thanks and got off the phone, eager to get back inside and make the rounds.

The rest of the night went by like a blur. The next morning was the same. I honestly couldn't even remember going to bed the night before. It was just past ten in the morning, and I was working with Owen, the guy I'd hired to be the manager. He'd been there each night, but tonight I planned on letting him close up on his own. It would be nice to get in bed before four in the morning. We were in the middle of doing inventory on the liquor when Alexis walked in the door.

I nearly dropped a full bottle of Grey Goose when I saw her. I caught it at the last millisecond and handed it to Owen. "Are you good to finish without me?" I asked.

Owen nodded. "Yeah, we're almost done anyway."

"Thanks," I said and rushed around the bar to greet Alexis.

I waved her over to the back, where my office was. She followed, and I closed the door behind us.

I spoke before she could say anything. "Alexis, I need to tell you what happened. It wasn't what you thought."

She held up her hand and said, "Kim told me."

"Great. But I still want you to hear it from me. No middle men."

She nodded, and I went through the whole story.

"...I had her thrown out and blacklisted. And that is, one hundred percent, the truth of what happened. I never, not in a million years, would have offered up this favor to shit on the agreement the very first night. As long as you're still good, I'm good. I'll follow all the rules, and keep things professional."

Alexis looked at me with narrowed eyes and asked, "Are you okay?"

I was caught off guard by the question. "What do you mean?"

Shrugging, she said, "I don't know, you seem sort of distant."

I knew it was true. I was trying to build up a bit of a wall between us. She only thought this was a game, an act, nothing more. I wanted to protect myself by not getting attached. Before last night, I'd started having real feelings for her, but after talking to Kim it was obvious that there was nothing reciprocal with Alexis.

I said, "Hey, I'm just playing a part. I want to make sure we do this right, and I keep my word."

A look that might have been irritation, or maybe hurt, flitted across her face. Before I had a chance to try and analyze it, she spoke again. "Well the next big thing is a family dinner on Friday. It's a family meet and greet before the wedding, so the inlaws can meet each other." She threw up her hands. "Which is bonkers since they all freaking met back when Tony and I dated, but whatever. It's also semi formal, since apparently my sister is dramatic. What a damned bride-zilla."

I pulled out my planner and marked it down on the calendar. "I'll be there. Pick you up an hour before dinner starts?"

She sucked in a deep breath. "Sounds good. I wanted to say sorry for not letting you explain."

I waved it off. "Hey, I understand. It looked pretty bad."

"No. I took it the wrong way. I'm used to getting looked over." She shrugged. "It stung, but I still shouldn't have ignored you like that." Standing, Alexis looked toward the door. "I need to go. I do want to say your place is awesome. I hope the whole week goes great. I'll see you Friday?"

She was opening the office door and stepping out when I said, "For sure."

The door closed behind her with a click. I sat there for several minutes thinking about what she'd said. *So, used to getting looked over.*

Damn it. I was a dick.

Chapter 7 - Alexis

The whole Idea of keeping this charade going was draining me. It made me feel like shit, even though it'd been a few days since I'd spoken to Sting. He'd acted so...cold?

No, he'd been nice, maybe just weird. It was obvious that this was all just a job to him. Honestly, my family wouldn't have been shocked to find me suddenly single again. Maybe that was the easiest way to go about this. We could have a breakup. It seemed more and more like the better option, especially with the fact that I was starting to like Sting. As in, *like* him.

Was that true? I had to ask myself that question multiple times a day. Was it really Sting I was starting to like, or was it this character he was playing. Maybe he wasn't anything like this in real life? From the moment I met him he'd been acting a part. Was it all for show?

I worked in the office of the school for a while, letting everyone else handle the kids. I needed a break to get my thoughts in order. After lunch I came to the conclusion that I needed to cut him out of my life. Stop things now before I ended up hurt. Before I *let* myself get hurt that is. I didn't think I'd be able to handle that again. Some dark part of my mind told me it would be better to be alone than to risk getting hurt like the last time.

One of the teachers leaned into the office. "Lex? You got a delivery."

"A what?" I couldn't imagine what might be delivered for me at work.

The teacher smiled. "Yeah. I hope he's hot," she continued in a whisper. "Because this is some romantic shit."

My eyes widened as I stood and hurried out of the office. In the lobby of the school, a young man stood holding a giant vase of flowers. In his other hand, he held an envelope. When he saw me he smiled, and I noticed he wore a uniform for a local florist. "Alexis?"

"Yes," I said warily.

He handed me the envelope and sat the flowers on a table near the door. "There you go. Have a great day."

I didn't even watch him leave. I gaped at the flowers. They were gorgeous and must have cost a couple hundred dollars from the size and quality. I ripped the envelope open and read:

Alexis,

I'm so sorry for the way I sounded Sunday. I didn't mean to come off sounding cold or callus. I know that must have upset you and I apologize. I want to make it up to you. Anything you want, just let me know. See you soon, hopefully.

Yours, Sting

I read the note three times, and each time I chewed at my lip harder, and harder, doing my best to keep myself from reacting. I needed to be clinical about this, emotionless. I had to look at things objectively and not let myself react. No matter what I did, I couldn't stop the little butterflies from fluttering in my stomach.

It was all I could do to get through the rest of the day at work and get home without texting him. I wanted to at *least* make him wait for my response. No longer able to stand it, I pulled my phone out after getting home and sent him a text.

Me: I got the flowers. They were beautiful. What did you have in mind?

Sting: Great.

Sting: What time do you usually go to bed? I don't want to keep you out late when you have to work in the morning.

I stopped and smiled despite myself. The fact that he had consideration for my time and my job made me feel good. I couldn't remember the last time a guy cared about that. Christ, I couldn't remember a guy *ever* caring. It was always about how much they could prove and do, with no thought about my time.

Me: I need to be home by 9.

Sting: Plenty of time. Do you want to meet me for dinner?

Me: Sure, why not?

Sting: Awesome. Have you ever been to that diner near where Kim used to live? It's probably a twenty minute drive.

Me: No, but I know where it is. I can meet you there.

Sting: An hour?

Me: See you then.

Sting: See you.

I changed quickly and was happy that he hadn't picked something fancy. For one, I really wasn't in the mood to get all done up after spending a day at work. And for another, it was much less pressure to go someplace low key.

I met him at the door of the diner, and as soon as we walked in I smiled. It was like something out of a movie from the fifties, and it smelled amazing. I did notice a few stares and glances as we approached the hostess podium. It took me a few seconds to realize why. Sting's shifter mark was on his jacket. For some people a human going on a date with a shifter was still taboo. Kind of the way people looked at same sex couples, twetny years ago, or interracial couples fifty years ago. It was stupid and ignorant, so I tried to ignore everyone. Sting seemed oblivious to it.

While we waited for a server Sting asked, "How was your week?"

I gave him a quick run down of the random stuff that had gone on. I made sure not to mention the fact that I had been about an inch away from ending things with him off and on all week.

"Well, I've been thinking about Friday night. It's coming up quickly, and I think we need to know more about each other if we are going to pull this off."

I nodded. "Agreed."

Sting laid his hands on the table. "Cool. Let's play twenty questions. I'll go first. What is your favorite color?"

I laughed and went along with it. We talked about our favorite sports, clubs we'd been in as kids, friendships, and our first jobs. We stayed away from anything too serious.

My family wasn't crazy invested in my life and they wouldn't care about Sting's. This was only about the things that would come up in general conversation.

"Why don't they want to know about what makes you tick? Seems pretty crazy to not want to know what your family is doing," Sting asked after we'd ordered.

I frowned and stirred my tea. "I'm different from them. I think it maybe makes them all uncomfortable with how opposite I am. It made me feel like an outsider growing up. Even in my own house. I've kind of learned to look past it."

Sting looked irritated. "Well, that's some horseshit. I don't think it's right that you should get used to people treating you like garbage. I know what that's like, but the fact that you've had to live with it your whole life is terrible. You deserve better than that."

I smiled sadly. "Thanks, you're right. I should try to think like that more often." I cleared my throat and redirected the conversation. "What about you? What's your past like?"

He looked a bit uncomfortable, and he seemed almost ready to shut down. Was it that bad? I wondered if I'd asked too much, probed too far already?

Before he could say anything I said, "Hey, no biggie. You don't have to share if it's too painful."

His brow furrowed and he said, "No, I'll tell you if it's necessary."

I bit my lip nervously, wondering what could be so bad. Now I desperately wanted to know.

Sting sighed. "It's not that I don't trust you with my story. It's just really dark and painful. I don't want that stuff rattling around in your head while we do this."

I reached out and touched his hand. "That is fine. Seriously. You don't need to tell me about it until you're ready."

The food came then, and after a few minutes Sting looked at me and smiled. "Thanks. For not pushing."

To lighten the mood, we started talking about our lives again. I learned how the Shifter clan worked. I also heard about all the drama the club had been through the last year or so. I told him about my friends, my job, and anything else I could think of. We talked for over an hour after we were done with our food.

It was a really great night. In fact, even though it was pretend, it was the best date I ever remembered going on.

After we paid the check, each of us paying our own way, Sting walked me out to my car. We were quiet on the walk. When we got to my car it was obvious Sting was a little hesitant about something, but he finally stepped forward and gave me a hug. He was much taller than me, at least eight or nine inches. I had to crick my neck to look up at him.

Seeing me do that he laughed. "I'm gonna start calling you Short Stuff."

Frowning, I gave him a pretend mad face and said, "I'm not short. I'm fun sized."

He looked at me with eyes that seemed to smolder after I said that. I almost melted under the heat of that gaze.

"How fun?" he whispered.

With those words, a flood of heat and lust rushed through me. I had to consciously control my breathing to keep from gasping. He kept his hand at the small of my back, and that little bit of contact made me want to shiver. My eyes locked on his, unable to look away as he pulled me closer. Pressed against his chest like that, I swore to the heavens I felt a bulge between his legs.

Sting spoke, his voice husky. "You can't look at me like that and think I won't react."

My heart was slamming in my chest. I wanted to say something, but my mouth wouldn't operate. He finally released me from my paralysis by stepping away. His fingers slid across my skin as he pulled his hand away from my back, and a rush of gooseflesh rippled up my arms and down my legs.

While I tried to pull myself together, Sting opened my door. "You better get home and get rested. It is a school night after all."

I stumbled over my own feet trying to get into the car, my face flushed with embarrassment. I mumbled. "Thank you," I said as I buckled up.

Before I closed the door, Sting leaned in. He moved lightning fast, but somehow it didn't seem rushed. He snaked a hand around and cupped my left cheek and turned my head gently toward him and kissed me. He kissed me like I'd never been kissed before. His tongue probed gently at my lips, and I greedily allowed it in. I twined mine around his as my nipples grew hard and my breath gasped. After *far* too few seconds, Sting pulled away.

I couldn't keep the smile off of my face. I was out of breath and doing my best not to pant. I looked at him and was about to ask where that had come from when I saw something that made my heart drop.

Across the street stood Tony. He must've been walking to his car when he'd seen us. He looked like he was pissed, and disappointment surged through me. I wanted to shove Sting to the ground. He hadn't really wanted to kiss me like that. He'd seen Tony and done what any dutiful actor should do, he'd played the part. It was all for show.

Before I was able to collect my thoughts, and say anything to Sting he said, "Get home safe."

He shut my door, and I started the car and drove away like a robot. I made it the whole way home, trying to be pissed at him. I was disappointed, but I had a hard time being angry. It had been such a great night. And that kiss? Jesus. It was all I thought about. My body was on fire.

After a while, a warmth and a slight pulse spread between my legs. I sighed as I pulled into my driveway.

I put my PJ's on, turned the lights out, and laid in bed, doing my best to not think about Sting, or the ache between my legs. My breath started to come heavy and fast as I succumbed to what was bouncing around my head. I slid a hand under the waistband of my pajamas. I was already wet as I closed my eyes and imagined how I wished the night had gone.

Sting was kissing me, like he had in the car, but I was on my bed. His hand slid down my chest, grazing my nipple through my shirt. I gasped and arched my back, pushing my crotch against his thigh. His lips slid down to my neck, licking gently at my throat as he slowly undid the fly of my jeans. He sat up and pulled my pants off in a flourish, and I sucked in a breath as he did the same to my panties. His hands were soft but strong as he clutched my butt and started kissing my legs, then my belly. His mouth moved closer and closer to my pussy. I was panting, almost hyperventilating when he blew a hot gentle breath across my clit.

I sighed and arched my crotch toward his face, desperate for his mouth to be on me. He obliged by taking his tongue slowly and luxuriously across my core. From the bottom all the way up to my clit, where he flicked the tip of his tongue. I couldn't take it anymore, and wrapped my fingers in his hair and pulled his face against me. His lips and tongue moved across me, and into me. I

groaned as he slid a finger inside me and slid his

mouth back and forth across my pussy.

I was getting close. An intense pressure built

within me. I thrust my hips against his face, feeling

his finger slide in and out of me. My body shook,

nearly vibrating. He wrapped his lips around my

clit and started sucking. It was gentle, but it was

enough. I screamed as my body was rocked by

wave after wave of pleasure, and he didn't stop.

Ten minutes later, I finally laid back,

breathing heavily, and exhausted. I smiled and

rolled over. I was asleep in minutes, my night

filling with dreams just like the fantasy I'd had.

Chapter 8 - Sting

My usual barber was able to fit me on Friday morning, a haircut and a beard trim. Lex made the whole thing seem like it wasn't a huge deal, but if I was going to do this thing I was going to make a good first impression. I tipped the barber well and headed out to a men's boutique clothing store that was between Forest Heights and Boise. They had really nice stuff, and I was pretty sure something there would work.

After about fifteen minutes of looking, the saleswoman at the boutique helped me into an outfit I liked. She let her hands linger on me a little longer than necessary as she measured me for a few quick alterations. I glanced down as she measured my waist. She gazed up at me. I saw the hungry look on her face and shook my head and rolled my eyes. There were some things about being a shifter that got old after a while.

Instead of looking back at her, I checked myself out in the mirror. I had to admit, I looked pretty damned good. I was actually looking forward to this little dinner.

I waited for thirty minutes for the alterations and took my clothes. I had a few hours left before meeting up with Alexis, so I stopped by the lounge to make sure Owen would be good. It would be the first night without me there at all, but he made it clear he felt fine managing solo.

When the time was right, I texted Alexis letting her know I was on the way. Ten minutes later I pulled up outside her place. Walking up to her door, I had the strange sensation of being nervous. It wasn't something I was used to when it came to women. I shook it off and rang the bell. When the door opened a few seconds later, it was all I could do to keep my mouth from hanging open.

She was fucking beautiful. She wore a bright yellow spaghetti strap sundress that came to mid thigh. It made her caramel brown skin look warm and inviting. Her heels made her at least four inches taller, and damn her legs were amazing. She'd pulled her curly locks back into a bun, but a few curls hung down and framed her face.

The bear inside me suddenly roared, demanding to be set free. I stepped forward and grabbed her by the hips, pulling her against me, my hands acting of their own accord. She wore minimal makeup, but I still didn't want to mess it up, so as badly as I wanted to kiss her I managed to hold back, by sheer force of will.

"You look...amazing." I said, trying to control my voice and keep from growling. I didn't totally succeed.

She looked at me with shocked amazement, no doubt about the way I was acting. I knew I was being more aggressive than I should have been, but I couldn't help myself. I leaned forward and gave her a gentle peck on the cheek. "Are you ready to go?" I asked.

"Uh." She shook her head like she was trying to clear it. "Yeah, yeah I'm ready. But come in for a picture first. I remembered you cleaned up well, but this?" She looked me up and down. "It's definitely picture worthy."

I laughed and followed her inside.

"We can put the pictures online, then it will seem more believable that we're dating. The whole damned world lives on the internet. I'm sure my sister is already suspicious that there aren't any pictures of us on my profile."

I nodded. "Yeah, makes sense."

I let Alexis play photographer for a while. She had us pose together, did several selfies, and one of us kissing, which made my heart leap into my throat. Finally, she put the phone on the table with a timer. She pressed against me and we smiled at the phone waiting for the flash. I stood there smiling like an idiot, trying to figure out how a woman so gorgeous, sexy, funny, and smart could possibly be single. It made no damn sense.

Alexis grabbed the phone and flipped through the pics, trying to find the best ones to post. I watched over her shoulder as she swiped through them.

I smiled and said, "Damn. We look good together.

I watched Lex's shoulders sag a bit and she sighed. It sounded like the saddest sound ever. "Yeah. We do."

Frowning, I wanted to ask why she seemed down all of a sudden, but we had a long night ahead, so I left it. It seemed strange that she would be so happy but then crash like that. Had I said something wrong?

In the car, Alexis plugged her parents' address into my GPS to keep from her having to give me turn by turn direction. We chatted about random things the whole drive. Nothing too serious. It was nice to relax and talk to someone about the little things that happen every day. Painting a picture of my daily life with words. I had to admit, it was strangely relaxing.

I turned the GPS off when we came to the gate that blocked off her parents' neighborhood from the road.

"This is a ritzy part of town. Don't think I've ever even been in here before," I said.

Alexis snorted. "Yeah. the Beverly Hills of Idaho. The code is pound, two, nine, seven, one, star."

I leaned out the window and punched the code, and waited for the gate to slide away. I drove into the neighborhood and cruised along slowly, trying not to gawk at the houses.

"That's it on the right," Alexis said, pointing.

I pulled up, put the car in park, and stared at the house in amazement. It was a mansion. I literally couldn't think of another word to describe it. It had to be at least ten-thousand square feet. Three stories and sprawling. There was a fucking fountain out front for fuck's sake.

I looked at Alexis, my eyebrows raised. "For real?"

She frowned sourly. "It's gaudy, I know. I'm sorry. And it is only my parents who live there. They don't need even half that thing. It's not where we grew up, that place was still big, but it felt more like a home than this monstrosity. About ten years ago Mom decided she needed a bigger house. Something to brag about to her country club friends, so my dad made this happen." She gestures toward the behemoth.

I shook my head, still trying to wrap my mind around it. I'd known her family was wealthy but this was next level. "What the hell does your Dad do for a living?"

Shrugging, Lex said, "He started as a programmer. Right before I was born he came up with some accounting program that he was able to sell for a lot of money. He invested that into his own company and then five years later came up with another program. I have to be honest, I have no idea what it does, but it got sold to Microsoft for...like...well it was a lot. That's all he does is churn out computer code all day."

I laughed getting out of the car. "I love my lounge, but I have to say I'm in the wrong damned business. I'm impressed."

Lex smiled as I opened her door for her. "You should be. That's their goal."

We laughed together as we walked up to the door. My hand found hers and she let me hold it. When she didn't pull away I did my best to hide a grin.

We walked up the pathway toward the door. I was surprised when the door opened just before we got there. A short older woman dressed in a classic maid's outfit smiled at us.

She said, "Alexis dear. They are all in the sitting room. Head on in."

I followed Lex inside and gaped at the floor. It looked like marble, honest to god marble. Who had real marble floors? We came to the sitting room, and a small group of people. My eyes darted around, glancing at each person.

I spotted the sister immediately. Not to be a dick, but she was not even remotely in Alexis's league, she was attractive, sure, but she wasn't even in the same area code.

Lex piped up. "Hey guys."

The room fell quiet as soon as she spoke and all eyes turned, nearly in unison, toward us. I bit the inside of my cheek to keep from laughing and rolling my eyes. The drama was thick. Had they practiced that before we'd gotten there?

Alexis was not having it though. "Can you guys stop being weird?"

The man, who must have been her dad, laughed and walked over to us.

He stuck out his hand to me to shake. "Welcome to my home. My name is Sam." I noticed the mother and sister didn't make any effort to introduce themselves to me.

"Nice to meet you, Sam. My name's Reese."

Sam looked at me and smiled warmly. "If you go by Sting, then Sting is who you are."

Bridget muttered into her mother's ear. "What kind of white trash name is that anyway? Sting?"

Thankfully, only my shifter hearing could pick up the whisper. I was glad Lex didn't have to hear that little jab. It didn't bother me, but it would have pissed her off. I realized that, not only did Lex have her sister beat in the looks department, but she also had her in the personality contest as well.

Sam took me by the arm and led me around the room introducing me to everyone in attendance. I liked Sam, which made it even more strange that he would have a daughter and wife as shrewish as the two women who were across the room talking to Lex now. I talked with everyone, but kept my ears open to the conversation happening with the three women.

Her mother said, "I don't know what you were thinking wearing something like that. Seriously Alexis?"

Bridget said, "Right. You don't have the shape to pull that off, and you know it. My god Lex what are you trying to prove?"

The mother added. "We need to get you a cardigan or something to cover up with. Especially since I can tell you've put on some weight."

My vision went red with anger. These two bitches were already on my last nerve. Lex was curvaceous and the curves were all in the right places. She didn't look like she'd just come from an anorexia boot camp like her mother and sister. I excused myself and strode across the room. I came up beside Lex, who already looked downcast and beaten down. We'd only been here five minutes, and they'd already done this to her. It pissed me the fuck off.

I slid a hand around her waist, surprising her, as she hadn't seen me come over. I said, "Well, I don't know about you ladies, but I like a woman with some curves." I looked at Lex. "Gives me something to hold on to."

Alexis shuddered under my hand, and her fingers snaked around my back, clutching me. I sensed her arousal, and my smile grew ever wider.

My shifter senses overloaded with messages from her body. I'd wondered if her attraction to me was real.

Now I knew. I really did have an effect on her. This had all started out as something pretend, a show for these stuck up snobs. Now I intended to make it something very much real. The looks of irritation and shock on her mother and sister's faces as I took Alexis in my arms and kissed her softly on the lips made me irrationally happy. This really was going to be a blast.

Chapter 9 - Alexis

My sister had been glaring at me the entire night. If looks could kill I'd be long dead, but I couldn't care less. After everything else I'd been through, a few awkward moments wouldn't bother me.

Tony finally showed up, and he wasn't speaking much to anyone. It looked like he was wound up tight like Bridget, and he kept his mouth shut, though I *did* notice a few sidelong glances he shot at Sting. It had been a really great night so far, to my surprise. Mom and Bridget had tried to body shame me. That little attempt had failed in epic fashion, thanks to Sting. Mom had been quiet too. I knew that wouldn't last, though. The other shoe would drop. I'd just enjoy myself until then.

Dad, as usual, was great. I hadn't expected anything less. I'd always wondered how he managed to live in this house with two people so...awful. Did I love my mom and sister? Yes. But did I like them? Bridget? No. Mom? Sometimes. Rarely.

Dad had never really said a lot when I was growing up, but there'd been a few times that the emotional abuse from Mom and Bridget got so intense even he'd noticed. He'd always stepped in to diffuse it. They'd always listened and backed down when Dad spoke. Of course, they had to. He was their bank. Literally, he was Daddy Moneybags for them.

The appetizers were almost done, and I smiled to myself knowing Sting's chef made better food than what I'd had here so far. My Mom would've lost her mind if she'd known.

The questions started as we sat at the table for dinner. Tony paid close attention to every word that came out of my or Sting's mouth. Like he was searching for us to screw up. The jerk.

How did we meet? How long have we been dating? All the questions we knew were coming. Sting took the lead and answered them. My eyes widened when he started going off script. Tony's gaze flicked over to me when I reacted, so I schooled myself into a happy smile. At least, I hoped it was happy-looking. I tried to mimick how I'd be if this was all real. Contet. Blissful. Not terrified and about to puke the dinner back up on the table.

Sting smiled and said, "How did we meet? Well, I have to say it was pretty fortuitous. I met her at a bar. I was slinging drinks one night and a mutual friend named Kim came in with Alexis in tow." He glanced over at me, smiling warmly. "When I saw her, she took my breath away."

I caught myself frozen and staring at him as he told the story. It was much better than what we'd rehearsed, and it made me warm and weak inside. Luckily, Tony's gaze was on Sting the entire time and he didn't notice my odd reaction.

"I worked up some confidence and went and made a proposition. She allowed me the opportunity to try and sweep her off her feet. Now I can't see myself without her." He finished and slid his hand into mine.

Everything he'd said sounded sincere. It made my chest ache. All those thoughts got pushed down, though. I had to keep reminding myself that this was a show, a game. I needed to guard my heart.

Mom piped up, her tone barely veiled condescension. "Mister...well, Sting? What do you do other than hang out in bars and sling drinks to drunkards?"

Dad placed a warning hand on her arm, but it wouldn't stop her. She wasn't being an overt bitch—yet.

Sting seemed unfazed. "Well, I was tending bar as research. You see, you can *think* you know what a customer wants, but until you've served them, you don't know for sure. I needed hands-on research so I was ready to open my own place." He took a bite, then grinned broadly. "It looks like it's working. We opened last Friday and it's been going great. I have an additional calendar for private events, birthday parties, wedding receptions, class reunions, stuff like that. We are already booked solid for the next three months."

I smiled, because it wasn't surprising. I chimed in. "It really is amazing. Everyone needs to take some time and come by and see it. I was there opening night and it really was like a Hollywood party or something. So, great."

Sting squeezed my hand, and a tingle went up my thighs as he continued speaking to everyone. "I've got plans for a few more enterprises. I'm letting the lounge get off the ground and running smoothly, and I'll start laying the groundwork for a few other businesses."

Mom looked confused. "Um, well, that's very commendable, but where are you getting the capital? Is there some investor or...another cash flow?"

I gritted my teeth, seeing where she was going with this. Anyone in town who didn't know better assumed the Forest Heights gang was a typical biker gang. Little did they know it held some of the saviest business men and intelligent people in the entire county, maybe even the state. Their money didn't come from drugs or prostitution. Nothing like that.

Sting stayed composed. "Well one of my good friends named Rhett Allen taught me a little about the stock market. I used what he taught me and with my own research and investment, I've done pretty well for myself. Everything I do is self funded. Even if I hadn't opened the business, I've done more than enough to live comfortably for the rest of my days."

I watched as Dad grinned to himself and nodded slightly, Sting continued. "I can live out whatever dreams I want. In fact, if there ever comes a time when Lex wants to venture out, maybe try something of her own, I'd be more than happy to support her."

Bridget, ready to explode already, scoffed. "What kind of goals would Alexis have? She doesn't really have aspirations. All she does is wipe butts and noses all day. I don't consider watching other people's rug rats as being a *career*."

I'd taken a lot of shit from her for multiple things my whole life, but I wouldn't back down when it came to my job."Bridget? How are you gonna call me out on my career when you don't have one yourself?"

Bridget looked like I'd slapped her, and Tony stopped chewing to glare at me. "I do. How dare you. I do have a career, a very successful one, I'll have you know."

I rolled my eyes. "Being a *social media influencer* at thirty years old is not a career. Like, what the hell does that even mean for cripes' sake? It *especially* isn't a career when all you do is post pictures of yourself in a bikini for a bunch of old pervs to stare at. Honestly, you should just drop the pretense and get your own porn site or join OnlyFans and be done with it. Drop trow and rake in some actual money."

Bridget's jaw dropped and Mom jumped in. "Alexis. Watch your mouth. This kind of behavior is not appropriate. You know better than this."

I chuckled humorlessly at my mother's hypocrisy. It was fine for Bridget to berate me, but I couldn't do the same? Sting grabbed my thigh and squeezed gently, letting me know he was there. I put my hand atop his and smiled at him. Seeing me oblivious to mom's chiding must have been too much for Bridget. She went into a full blown melt down.

She started screaming, honest to god screaming, right there at the table. "You are such a bitch. This is why Tony left your high and mighty ass back then. Christ, it's why he was cheating on you all through college. You didn't even know that he was fucking misserable with you. How could he want to be with someone so trashy and bitchy?"

I felt it before I heard it, a deep trembling rumble deep in my own chest. At first I thought it was an earthquake. Then I realized it was Sting. He was growling, and everyone went silent. I watched the color drain from my sister and mother's faces. Even as a lump formed in my throat, hurt and anger brought me to the brink of tears.

Sting leaned forward, locking his eyes on Bridget. "I understand that this is supposed to be a celebration of your and Tony's wedding. I get that this is supposed to be about you. It seems..." He smiled without humor. "That you are used to things always being about you. But the fact that you are marrying Alexis's sloppy seconds does not give you the right to speak to her that way. You may be used to getting your way. But in this? You will learn." He slammed his palm down on the table. "I will not sit back and allow anyone, *anyone.*" He glanced at Mom. "To disrespect Alexis in my presence. I hope you all understand that, and make the appropriate choices in the future, and watch your mouths."

He turned to me then. "Do you want to leave?"

I nodded, the burn of tears already stinging my eyes. I knew they were coming, but I hated crying in front of these people. They didn't deserve to see me upset.

We both stood and Mom said, "Alexis it's rude to leave in the middle of dinner."

Sting rounded on her, the movement catlike in it's speed. Mom jerked in her chair as though he slapped her. "No ma'am," he said quietly. "It is rude to treat your own daughter like she is a smear of dogshit on your shoe, one that has somehow ruined your day.

Mom gasped and put a hand to her chest. Through the blur of tears I saw Dad, his face a mask of disappointment. Thankfully, he was directing it at Mom and Bridget, not me.

Dad looked at Sting. "Son?"

Sting turned to him, his body tense, ready to defend me again.

Dad said, "Sting, my daughter is lovely. And her new dress is beautiful. Please don't let it go to waste. Take her somewhere nice for dinner so that she can get this." He turned a withering glare on Mom. "*Display,* out of her mind."

Sting smiled, surprised. "I'll do that."

Without another word, he wrapped an arm around me and led me from the house. I leaned against him as he guided me to the passenger door, and I slid in, the tears dripping from my face. He got in and pulled away from the house, silent, letting me cry for a few minutes.

Finally he spoke up, his voice heavy with emotion. "I'm sorry I snapped like that. I just...I couldn't sit there and let them keep going on and on like that. You do not deserve to be treated like that."

I wiped at my face as the gate opened to let us back out. The tears had stopped, and the sadness had been replaced by something else. This man, a man I'd only known for less than two weeks, had done what no one else ever had. He'd stood up for me, protected me. Put the fear of god into my mother, and roasted my sister in front of everyone. I wanted to thank him. No...I *needed* to thank him. Words weren't enough for what he'd done for me.

"Pull over," I said.

Sting glanced at me. "Do what?"

"Pull over, please."

"Uh, okay. Are you alright?" he said, pulling onto the shoulder.

He was putting the car in park as I unbuckled my seat belt.

"Do you need to walk a bit? Get fresh air?"

Without answering I crawled up into my seat and then threw my leg across his waist and settled into his lap, straddling him. I looked up, feeling as surprised as I probably looked, and I kissed him. I kissed him hard, and with every fucking thing I had in me, my fingers twining in his hair. The first second or two he sat rigid, shocked, but then his body relaxed and he returned the kiss. His tongue greedily slid into my mouth. His hands slid across my back and finally down to my ass, where he clutched me tightly and pulled me close. It was obvious how hard he'd become. It pressed through his pants and my body shivered in pleasure.

I finally pulled away, breathless. Sting let his head fall back onto the head rest and he put a hand to his forehead. He looked like someone had told him some little bit of unbelievable information.

He gasped. "Well, what was that all about?"

I laughed and slid my hands across his chest. "No one has ever stood up for me like that. Not even my dad. I wanted you to know how much it meant to me. There was only one way I could think of to say thanks."

He laughed and cupped my face, pulling me in for another kiss, then said, "You can thank me any time, any where."

I sighed and some of the sadness returned. "I'm sorry about all that. They are usually dicks, but I didn't really think it would be that bad."

Sting asked, "Well do you think you're off the hook now? Is Bridget gonna kick you out of the bridal party?"

"Nope, I won't get that lucky. She's getting this sick thrill of marrying Tony and rubbing my face in it. Honestly, I wouldn't be surprised if she takes a picture of them fucking on their wedding night and texts it to me. Just to see my response. But at this point I don't really want to be a part of it. I may bow out myself. It would get you out of having to pretend to be my boyfriend."

Sting surprised me by laughing and saying. "Well, the good news is I don't really feel like I need to pretend anymore. At least not after I jumped your Mom and sis from trying to call you fat."

I shook my head quickly, trying to clear my thoughts. "Wait...what? What do you mean?"

His hand came up and a finger traced the line of my jaw, and electricity coursed through my neck all the way down to my breasts.

"I mean, I want you. I want to date you for real."

I want you? The ache in my chest was unlike anything I'd ever had in my life. Like a hole inside me was suddenly filled.

"Are you being serious right now?" I asked, my voice quavering.

He grinned. "I am. What do you think?"

"I...I..." I felt like an idiot, but I physically could not form words. My mind had blown a fuse.

Sting kissed me again. It focused my thoughts back on him, and not the shock of what he'd said.

"It's okay," he said. "You can take some time to think it over. But right now I have one task and one task alone."

"Yeah?" I asked, still dazed.

"I need to get some meat into you."

I frowned at him then laughed as I shook my head. "You really shouldn't go with the double entendre."

He shrugged. "I thought it was funny."

We sat, an hour later, in a steakhouse. Sting was happily eating his rare ribeye, while I worked on a filet. He didn't push or ask questions. He just let me be in my head for a while. Work things out.

I really didn't get why he would want to be with me.

After finishing my meal I looked at him. "Okay, why do you want to date me? For real?"

He looked at me like I was crazy. "Um...let's see. You're beautiful, sweet, great personality, funny." A smile bloomed on my lips and I didn't try to hide it. "On top of all that, you are hot as fucking hell. Plus it seems like my bear is pretty obsessed with you."

I leaned back, surprised, and asked, "What does that mean?"

He put his knife and fork down and wobbled his head back and forth, looking like he was trying to find the right description.

At last he said, "Your smell. The smell of you."

Subconsciously, I pulled my arms close, trying to close off my armpits.

He laughed. "No, not like that. The smell of all of you." He moved his hands, gesturing to my whole body. "It drives me *and* the bear mad. It's the first time it's ever happened to me. All I know is that I want you. I want the chance to maybe see if there's anything real here." His face softened. "I totally get it if you aren't ready. I would like you to at least give it some thought before telling me to get lost for good."

Nodding I said, "Okay, I will. I promise." It was unlikely I'd be able to think about anything else.

He didn't press it like most guys would have. He just smiled at me and nodded, going back to his steak. After dinner, he drove me home. I went over what he'd said the whole way. I was still thinking about it as he walked me up to my door. He pulled me close for a goodnight kiss. It wasn't passionate like the one in the car earlier. It was sweet, gentle, and warm. It felt like home.

I got ready for bed a little while later,

thoughts and images still whirling through my

head. I laid down in bed, thinking about Sting.

About what happened tonight. Wondering if I was

really ready to start something real with this man.

A man who really wanted me. Me and nothing

else.

Chapter 10 - Sting

It had been over a week since I'd seen Mom, and I knew I needed to get out there and visit her. I decided to head out late Sunday morning to have lunch with her. I arrived right before noon and Mom had put out the usual Sunday spread I remembered from my childhood. Chicken salad sandwiches, macaroni salad, a bowl of chips, and fresh baked cookies. It was simple, but damn was it a nice sight.

Mom handed me a plate with a little of everything and said, "Sweetie, I really wish I could have been there for the opening. I couldn't talk myself into it. Didn't think it was the *scene* for a

sixty-five year old woman."

I bit into a sandwich and could almost taste

the nostalgia. I chuckled and said through a full

mouth. "Mom. You would have been welcomed

with open arms. I would have given you the whole

VIP treatment. Rivers of champagne. Mountains

of caviar."

She swatted me playfully, laughing. "Oh,

quit. Even if I wasn't there to see you, it still

makes me proud to see you so successful."

I reached up and squeezed her arm.

"Thanks. It really does mean a lot coming from

you, Mom."

She reached for a handful of chips, and looked at me with *the* look. She was about to ask me something. I knew from decades of experience that she was going to pretend like she was being subtle, when in reality she was going to be anything but.

"So." She paused and made a face like something had just occurred to her. "Your aunt called me yesterday. She said you've been seen around town with a pretty little lady. Your aunt said she didn't know her, and was positive she was a *human* girl."

I put my fork full of macaroni salad down and leaned back, groaning. "Oh, geez. Here it comes."

Mom raised her eyebrows. "Now, now. It's not like that. I'm not a bigot. I've never cared whether a person is human or shifter. Not even a little bit." She got a sad look on her face. "It's a little disappointing that I won't get to be a grandma."

I gave Mom a playcating look. "Mom, Grizz has a kid. Shit. He's got a kid *and* another on the way. Both with a human woman. It does happen sometimes. Not often, but it does happen. It could happen for us too."

I frowned and slapped a hand on my foreheads "Wait, Mom. What are we talking about here? Me and Alexis aren't even an official couple, and somehow you've got me talking about babies?"

Mom laughed a maniacal laugh, and whacked me on the shoulder. "You *must* really like that girl."

I sighed, picking at my food. I couldn't really deny that. I liked the hell out of her.

I said, "Yeah, okay. I do like her. Like, a lot. So, does my bear. It's like a wild animal inside me when I'm around her."

Mom gave me a serious look, then smiled and said, "It sounds like you've found your mate."

I had to admit, it had crossed my mind a few times since Friday night. Hutch and Grizz had told me what it was like when they were ready to claim their ladies. All the signs were there for me too. If someone had asked me how I would feel about this six months ago, I would have been irritated. Now? Now, the lounge was open and running smoothly, I had time. I had time to work on my love life. I could actually focus on other things. One of the things I really wanted to focus on was Lex.

Mom brought me out of my thoughts, and tanked my mood. "In other news. I need to tell you he called again."

I tensed up and started shaking my head.

"Reese, please. I think it would be good for you to sit down with him and talk." I took a breath to speak but she held up a hand to silence me.

"Reese, don't think I've forgotten all the things he put us through. I haven't. In fact, I remember more than you do. I've forgiven him, because if I didn't? Well if I didn't, then I would have never moved on. I never found the love of my life, no. I *am* happy, though. My son is healthy and happy too. You're thriving, and living your dreams. It's all I ever hoped for when we moved to Forest Heights. I want you, *us*, to finally heal."

She got up and hugged me then. It took everything I had to keep from crying.

I wrapped my arms around her and said, "I'm thankful for all the sacrifices you made for us Mom. I really am, but I am healed. I don't need to speak to Dad to do that. Please, tell him to stop

calling."

Mom pulled back, a few tears in her eyes and

nodded reluctantly. "Okay." She squeezed my

shoulders. "Okay, if he calls again, I'll tell him."

The drive home, I tried to keep my mind off of

Dad. Instead, I thought about Lex. I hadn't heard

from her in a couple of days, but I didn't want to

push things. I 'd let her know how I felt. My ball

had been served. I just had to wait for the return,

if there was one. I hoped I'd hear from her by the

end of the day.

I made a run out to the lounge to check on

Owen and see how things had gone so far this

weekend. I found him sitting at the bar going through receipts.

He glanced up. "Hey boss. How goes it?"

"Good. How were things the last couple of nights?"

Owen put his work aside and grinned. "Really good. Just as busy as last weekend. Starting to see a lot of regulars."

I smiled. Things were going well. I asked, "What about Reck? How was his first weekend?" I probably should've been here for it, but oh, well. I'd feel guilty about it if it hadn't gone well.

Owen's face crumpled into a confused frown. "Reck? Who's...Oh. Trey. Trey did great, man."

I winced, realizing I'd totally forgotten he didn't want to go by anymore. Christ, that was going to be hard to get used to.

"Sorry, yeah, Trey. He did good?"

Owen laughed. "Dude is a huge hit with the ladies. I think he made more tips than the whole rest of the staff combined last night."

Trey'd had a great personality, if a little volatile, before all the shit had gone down with Grizz's kid last year. After that, he'd become a shell of himself. It was nice to hear the old Trey was coming back, even if it was under another name.

"Awesome. I'm going to go to the office and check the weekend numbers and inventory real fast."

Owen nodded. "Sure, everything is up to date in the spreadsheets."

I spent fifteen minutes checking over the numbers. After seeing them, I made my way out with a bigger smile. Things were going *well*. Maybe my time table on some of my other ventures might move up, if revenue stayed like this.

I was almost to the door when it opened and Bridget walked in. I stopped in my tracks, irritation wiping away the good mood I'd been in. I was in no disposition to deal with her and whatever shit she was bringing into my place. I was, however, a professional. I put on my brightest smile and walked forward meeting her. "Bridget? Surprised to see you here. What can we do for you?"

I watched her glance around. The shock on her face told me that my place was not what she'd expected. She'd probably assumed it was a hole in the wall with hay and peanut shells on the floor. She was impressed, grudgingly anyway.

She finally pushed a strand of hair from her face and said, "You need to talk to my sister."

I arched an eyebrow at her. "Why would I do that?"

She stomped her foot. "Because. She called me and told me she wasn't going to be in the wedding."

Her voice was whiny, and it made my skin crawl hearing her. "Well it serves you right. You treat her like shit and you think she should, what? Thank you? You fucked her ex, got engaged to him, and rubbed her face in it? Why the hell would she want to be part of your big day? You are grade 'A' crazy, lady. You get some kind of thrill out of hurting your sister, right?"

Bridget's face went red and I could tell she wanted nothing more than to slap the shit out of me. "You don't know anything about me."

Rogue had done some digging and found out that Tony had been trying to find out about me. He'd been asking around town. Ol' Tony was trying to get dirt on me.

"You should just worry about yourself and your boy Tony. You both need to leave Alexis alone."

She tossed her hair. "Tony is totally over Alexis. Totally. He has me now so why would he want to even think about her?"

I really wanted to knock this bitch down a peg or two. I wasn't usually the type to rain on people's parade, but she was asking for it. I wanted to tell her how Tony had tried to warn me off of dating Lex. Though, that might get Alexis

pulled deeper into this shit storm.

I opened my mouth to tell Bridget to leave

Lex alone, but before I spoke a pleasant warmth

spread through my chest, and a scent I recognized

hit me. I smiled as Lex walked through the doors

of the lounge. She almost slid to a stop seeing

Bridget here. Her eyes bounced from her sister to

me and back again. Bridget looked ready to tear

the place apart.

Alexis looked at me. "What the hell is going

on?"

Before I could answer Bridget spat. "You're

such a selfish bitch, you know that? Backing out of

my wedding? Who the fuck do you think you are?"

I let out a growl and was pleased to see Bridget step back from me, her eyes fearful.

I whispered, "I think I've already discussed with you that I won't have you disrespect Alexis in front of me. I'm not going to tell you again."

Alexis stepped over and placed a hand on my bicep. "It's fine." She turned to her sister. "Bridget, I meant what I said. I am not going to be at the wedding. That's final."

Bridget was pissed. She looked like she might have a stroke. "You'll regret this."

Brushing past Lex, I pointed my finger at Bridget. "Do not threaten her. You hear me, you little brat?"

Bridget stomped her foot again and spun around, storming out. I stood for several seconds letting my temper ease off. Once I was in control, I turned back to Alexis.

She shook her head. "I'm sorry about that. I didn't mean to bring all this shit down to your place."

I didn't care about all that. All I wanted was one thing. I stepped forward and took her in my arms and kissed her. She didn't fight, but almost seemed to melt into me. I deepened my kiss and heard her moan. After several seconds I pulled away.

Smiling at her, I said, "I assume, since you're here, you did a little thinking?"

She nodded. "I've always had terrible luck with relationships, but I want to try again. With you...like a real one, not pretend. Do you still want to?"

I grinned like a school boy. I didn't really have the words to express what I wanted to say. So, instead I pulled her to me again and kissed her senseless.

Chapter 11 - Alexis

My phone had buzzed at least three dozen times over the last twenty four hours. All of them from my mom and Bridget. I'd had to turn my phone to silent because I couldn't take it anymore. Every message was basically the same. I was being selfish, I was not thinking about the big picture, I was making the wedding about me instead of my sister, I was jealous. Over and over. My mom's messages were attempting to guilt trip me, Bridget's were spiteful for no reason.

Considering I'd always been the odd one out in our family, it didn't hurt as much as I figured it would have. If someone told me this would happen three weeks ago, I would have assumed I'd be in a fetal position crying my eyes out? Now? I realized that's how they were, and I couldn't take it to heart. I wasn't special, they would have reacted the same way to anyone doing this to Bridget.

My phone buzzed again. "Fuuuuck," I moaned.

I sat up and grabbed it, wondering what new load of shit Mom or Bridget was going to send me. Instead I saw it was a message from Dad.

Dad: Hey kid. I want you to know that you need to do what's best for you. Your well being is just as important as your sister's. If being a part of this wedding is causing you more harm than good, then you shouldn't have to be part of it. I love you.

I teared up as I read his message. It meant the world to me that he supported me. It would have been nice if he'd done more over the years to stand up to my mom and sister, but a little was better than nothing. If it had been all three of them against me, I had no idea what I would have done. Just cut total ties with my family? Maybe. Probably would've been my only option.

I made it to work about an hour later, and Kim was there, chomping at the bit to ask how the dinner on Friday went.

She pulled me aside. "I thought you'd text or call me about it."

I sighed and said, "Sorry, I meant to. It was a total disaster. Name calling, screaming, the whole nine yards."

Kim's shoulders slumped. "Oh sweetie I'm so sorry. That fucking sucks."

"Yeah, it does. But...something good came of it." I tried to suppress my smile.

Kim raised an eyebrow, and I told her what Sting had done at the dinner. The way he'd stood up for me and got me out of there, the kiss on the way home. Then how he'd berated my sister at the lounge, and how we'd decided to give it a shot as a couple.

Kim squealed in excitement and wrapped me in a hug. "I *knew* there was something between you. I knew it."

I laughed despite myself. "I do have some reservations, though," I said, "I've only had one true relationship, and that went to shit. I've got all kinds of baggage and issues. I'm worried that once he sees the real me he'll run for cover. Or maybe I'm scared that I don't deserve to be happy, and I'll try to subconsciously screw this up before it really starts."

Kim looked me in the eye. "You've been through some shit, yes. It's understandable that you're hesitant, but you need to get out of your head and let this flow where it wants. Don't pressure yourself or Sting. Live in the moment, and enjoy hanging with a really cool guy." She grinned then. "Cool and *really* hot."

I snorted a laugh. "Okay, yeah. I'll give it a try. Thanks."

The day went by pretty quickly. The one thing about little kids, they never give you any time to stew in your thoughts. It was nonstop all day, and it seemed like the end of the day came quickly. I finished cleaning up and waved to Kim and everyone else as I headed out the door. But then I pulled up short. Sting was waiting for me out on the sidewalk.

Blinking in surprise I couldn't help but grin. "What the heck are you doing here?"

Sting smiled back. "I'm taking you to dinner. What does it look like?"

I raised my eyebrows, and playfully walked past him. "You do know there's this thing called *asking* right?"

He grabbed my hand and grinned mischievously, pulling me up short. "You would have said yes."

Rolling my eyes at his audacity, I walked back and let him pull me in for a kiss.

"I'll bring you back to your car after dinner. I promise."

He took me to the best pizza place in town. It wasn't crazy busy, being a Monday night. It seemed like we almost had the place to ourselves.

Sting bit into a bread stick and asked, "What are your plans for the week? I was going to see if you wanted to go to the pack meet coming up. It'll be fun, I'd love to have you there."

I made a face. "Oh geez. That's intimidating. Are you sure I'd be, I don't know, welcome?"

Chuckling, he responded sweetly. "Yeah, we may be shifters, but we're pretty laid back. Besides, there will be a lot of other humans there too. Kim and Zoey to start." He looked at me with smoldering playful eyes. "Plus, my bear is getting impatient to meet you."

"I have to be honest," I said. "That sounds kind of scary. I've never seen you, or any shifter actually *shift* before. I mean, I've seen it in movies and stuff, but never in person." Deep down, the idea of seeing it was a little thrilling. "Tell me how it all works. That might help me decide. Like, are you still in control? Is it still *you* when you're the bear?"

Sting noded. "Yeah, it's still me. My instincts are more basic. I'm closer to nature than the human world, but I still have my own thoughts. I can stop myself from, say, mauling someone or overreacting to stimuli. In all, it's like a highly evolved grizzly bear."

"Well how does this bear feel about me? You keep saying he wants to meet me."

He glanced down at the table, and a nervous look came over his face. After a few seconds he said, "Okay, so, here's the deal. I probably shouldn't tell you this. It might freak you out, but oh well. Basically the bear inside every shifter kind of chooses a mate. It picks the person it wants to claim as their mate. There's an intense desire to be near them, around them, anything. Also an overwhelming need to protect them. It's...it's part of the reason I was ready to rip your Mom and sister's heads off Friday night. It's kind of like a territorial thing." He glanced down at my neck. "The bear wants to leave a mark, but usually hickeys and things like that can satisfy it in the short term."

My whole body flooded with heat. My skin flushed and I was a little embarrassed.

Sting could see my reaction. "Yeah, it's a lot, I know." He smiled. "It's not for everyone, but it's just our nature."

I nodded thinking about it. I'd never in my life been this desired by anyone. Human or shifter. I had a sudden thought and had to voice it.

"So, is that the only reason you want to be with me is because the bear wants me?"

Sting leaned forward lighting quickly, sensing what I was implying. He grabbed my hands and looked into my eyes.

"The bear only reacted because I allowed it, because it sensed what I was feeling. I already had a natural connection to you. The bear simply agreed."

I sighed with relief.

Sting continued. "*I* want you, my bear has no control over what I want. No more than I can control who he does. Though he rarely voices an opinion. Can I ask how you feel about me?"

The question caught me off guard. I was still caught up on who else the bear had liked.

Thinking about what he'd asked me, I was scared

to fess up to the emotions going through me.

Though, I should voice it. He'd already opened

up about how he felt, it wouldn't be fair for me to

keep it inside. "I'm very attracted to you. I love

how driven and determined you are." I grinned

and blushed. "You're sweet, funny, and really hot.

You also kind of scare me, because it would be

really easy for you to break my heart. If I gave my

heart to you, that is, it would be easy." Oh, yeah.

Awkward.

He looked at me, and was silent for several

seconds, then said, "You have the same power

over me."

My eyes widened. Was he serious? Surely not. Yet the look on his face said he knew it was true.

Sting said, "How about this? Let's avoid the unnecessary drama most relationships go through by being open with our feelings. Communication is key right?"

It made me smile hearing him say that. It sounded like a great idea. "I think I can do that."

Sting leaned across the table and kissed me, then said, "I think we'll be great together."

After we'd finished dinner Sting did as promised and drove me back to my car. He glanced at me after putting the car in park.

"So...are you gonna come to the pack meet on Friday?"

"I wouldn't miss it for the world," I said.

Sting laughed and leaned in to kiss me again, but stopped before getting to my lips.

He sniffed his nose once and growled. "You've got to be fucking kidding me."

Frowning, I asked, "What?"

"Douchebag Tony is here."

I spun around in my seat trying to see him. Finally I watched him get out of a car about a block away.

I looked back at Sting. "How the hell did you do that?"

He tapped the side of his nose. "I memorize scents. Everyone has one that is just a little different from everyone else. Most shifters can do it, but mine is super sensitive, even for us."

Sting got out of the car and came around to open my door, ready to walk me to my car.

Tony was ten feet from us when he said, "Lex can I talk to you?"

Trying to ignore him I said, "Don't know what there is to talk about honestly."

Tony glanced down at his feet. He looked nervous. It was not something I usually saw from him. He was usually a cocky ass who was never wrong.

"It's about what Bridget said at dinner the other night, okay?" he said, still not looking me in the eye.

I stopped dead, tugging at Sting's arm to make him stop too. "Oh, you mean the fucking truth bomb she dropped? Where she let me know that all that time we were in college, and I thought we were gonna get married, but you were out night after night shoving your dick into whatever girl you could find? Is that what you wanted to talk about? If so, it doesn't matter anymore does it? Don't worry about it. You did what you did and there's no going back. It's in the past." I pulled away from Sting and poked a finger into Tony's chest. "You're marrying my sister. You should be focusing on your wedding. Focus on the fucking miserable future you're going to have with her."

I stepped back and hooked my arm around Sting, wondering if Tony would have a response. It was invigorating to tell him my real feelings. Tony looked torn about something, which made me confused. Was he wanting to apologize? Call me out for some shit he thinks I did? Try to win me back?

"Tony, let it go," I said wearily.

Tony took a step toward me. Sting slid an arm around me, gently positioning me behind him. He growled deeply and eyeballed Tony. Tony slid to a stop so fast he almost slipped and fell.

His shoulders sagged and he asked, "Lex can't we talk in private?"

Sting spoke up. "Tony, she said she didn't want to talk. Respect that and go home."

Tony's face flushed in anger. "Hey man. You don't speak for her. Let her make her own decisions."

"I know I don't. I'm literally only repeating what she said. That she doesn't want to talk to you. If you were a decent human being and not a piece of shit you'd stop dragging all this crap out and let her move on with her life."

I knew the look Tony had on his face. He was pissed, and if he could have, he would have tried to jump Sting. I'd seen him get in fights for less in college and high school. Thankfully, he still had enough self awareness to know better.

Tony leaned around Sting and spoke directly to me. "Are you really gonna settle for *this*?" He sneered waving a hand at Sting.

I pushed Sting out of the way gently and said, "Settling? That's what I would have done if I'd stayed with you. You need to let me live my life."

Tony shook his head and looked at me in disgust. "You are making such a big mistake." He turned and stormed back to his car, calling over his shoulder. "The biggest mistake of your life."

Sting stood rigid staring at Tony until he drove away, then turned to me. "He's going to keep being a problem. I know it. I'm going to follow you home, okay? I just want to make sure you get there safely."

I didn't think Tony would harm me. That wasn't how he worked, but I wanted to give Sting some peace of mind. "Okay, yeah. That's fine."

The whole drive home I was much more secure with the rumble of a motorcycle behind me. I kept checking my rear view mirror and saw Sting's hair flying from under his helmet. It was nice to have someone watching over me, I decided.

At my house, Sting walked me up to the door. I noticed that he kept looking around, he must have been looking for Tony. I didn't really blame him for being on high alert. Not after

everything his clan had been through the last little

bit. I unlocked the door and turned to Sting. He

leaned forward, a hand on my cheek, and kissed

me deeply. Every time I kissed him it felt like the

first time, butterflies in my stomach.

"I'll call you tomorrow," he said, then

sniffed the air several times. He looked satisfied

when he said, "Good night, Lex. See you soon."

Chapter 12 - Sting

Tony. I couldn't get that asshole off my mind, even with him being the last thing I wanted to think about. My gut told me I needed to keep an eye on him. I generally tried to listen to my gut. It wasn't often wrong, considering those gut feelings were usually my bear, keeping me in line and ahead of situations.

I didn't like how he kept trying to pop up and tell Alexis what to do with her life, and how to live it. Especially since it seemed like he still wanted to be a major part of her life. Which, in my opinion, was double fucked seeing as how he was marrying

Lex's sister. He'd let her go, then thrust himself back in the picture with Bridget. It was borderline psycho. Was he just trying to keep control over his ex? That wasn't going to fly.

All of my suspicions led me to schedule a meeting with Rouge. It was time to get some help with this guy and what was the point of being in a clan like mine if I couldn't get a little assistance now and again? I wanted to see what else we could do to keep tabs on him.

Rogue and I met up at the clubhouse for lunch around noon. Rogue walked in carrying a giant bag full of burritos from a Mexican joint in town. Nice. The smell reached me before he did, and my stomach rumbled.

"Hope you like steak burritos, bro," he said as he sat down with me.

I grinned and gladly took the offered wrapped food. "Sure dude, I'm freaking starving." I ripped it open and took a big bite, not waiting to dig in on the conversation too. "So," I said around the food, which was amazing, "about this guy messing with Lex?"

Rogue pulled a foil wrapped burrito out for himself and sighed deeply. "Man, I am staying away from human women. Between you and Hutch and Grizz? It seems like they are *a lot* of work, and trouble. I've never been this busy." He snarled his lip as he opened a packet of hot sauce.

I threw my head back and laughed. It did seem like everyone in the clan who started dating humans had found themselves in some type of shit or another. But it was totally freaking worth it so far. Just being around Alexis was a reward.

Rogue went on. "If I start making googly eyes at some human chick please talk me out of it. Turn my head toward some hot shifter lady and save me some grief."

Taking a bite of my food I said, "I'll try to keep that in mind. But for real, this Tony dude?"

Rogue raised his eyebrows tilted his head back and forth, thinking.

"I think I can maybe hack his phone account, try to see what kind of calls he's making and whatnot. That could help a little, to keep tabs on him. I mean if it starts to look really crazy we could get the guys together and put a watch on Alexis."

I frowned. That seemed like a lot. Maybe too much. "Man, I don't want to go that far yet. I did that for Hutch with Kim, and while I was happy to do it...it was fucking exhausting. I don't want anyone in the crew to have to do that unless it's absolutely necessary."

Rogue and I talked for a while, eating, bouncing around ideas. I decided that having him watch Tony's online and phone activity would be enough for now. A few hours later, when I was back at my place, happy to be doing something more, I checked in on Lex.

She answered on the third ring. "Hey."

Damn, her voice was like... soothing somehow. "Well, hello there pretty lady. I called to check in on you. Make sure everything is okay."

She blew out a breath and said, "I literally had to block every one of my family members, except Dad. Mom even had some of my aunts and cousins texting and calling me asking to reconsider. Just full on harassment."

I could hear how stressed she was. Damn it, I wanted to see her again, but I didn't want to crowd her or overwhelm her. It'd be great if I freaked her out and sent her packing before I had a chance to get things rolling. I knew she would be at the pack meet Friday, so I needed to be patient.

We stayed on the phone for several minutes, just chatting. She seemed much less anxious by the time we got done. "Thanks, Sting," she said.

"For what?" I want to tell her I'd do anything for her. I didn't want to scare her away though.

"For everything. See you Friday?"

"Wouldn't miss it."

By the time Friday came I was about ready to explode with energy, and I wasn't the only one. Every one of the guys was buzzing, ready for the run later. I was extra pumped and jittery though, knowing Alexis was going to be there. It must have shown.

"You good big guy?" Hutch called over to me as we stood outside waiting for everyone to arrive.

Damn. Here it came. They were going to have to get in some razzing time. I should've expected it. "Yeah, why?" I tried to sound casual.

Rogue chimed in, of course. "Because you look like a high school kid waiting on his prom date."

I waved them off. I didn't mind the teasing. Hell I probably would have said the same thing if I was in their shoes, but before I said anything I sensed Alexis.

My soul sighed in releaf as I recognized her car when it pulled in with several others. She got out a second after parking, and I smiled, unable to stop myself. Too bad she looked apprehensive and nervous, cause I was thrilled as hell for her to be here. I played it cool as I walked toward her waving.

She saw me and a huge smile lit up her face. Her happiness at seeing me was enough to break my cool demeanor. She was happy to see me! Genuinely pleased. Hell, yes. I jogged the rest of the way and pulled her into a kiss so hard and deep when we finally broke away we were both breathless. I heard the catcalls and whistles the rest of the clan sent our way, but we both ignored them.

Lex took a deep breath. "I did not expect that. It was a really nice way of saying hello."

I shrugged a little embarrassed. "I guess I missed you this whole week." It was true. Not said for anyone else's benefit.

She looked surprised that I would say that, as well as touched. It made my heart hurt seeing this amazing woman actually be shocked that someone would miss her. It was mind boggling, and made me hate the people in her life who had made her feel that way her whole life.

She ran a hand across my chest and up to cup my cheek. "I missed you too."

Grinning, I took her by the hand. "Come on, Kim and some of the other ladies are over by the fire."

We sat down together and waited a couple minutes until Grizz came out, Rainer trailing behind him. Grizz stood up on a large stump and faced the crowd, who went silent.

Grizz spoke. "Friends. It's good to see everyone. We have a lot to be happy for. Tonight is a night we all look forward to, and I for one am not going to hold us up. Let's do the damned thing."

The men in the crowd roared in agreement. Alexis jerked in surprise, and then laughed.

I took her hands and asked, "Are you ready to meet my bear?"

She looked nervous, but nodded. "Yeah, I think so."

I led her away from the rest of the group, trying to find a private space. I just wanted to make sure she understood what was about to happen.

"I don't want you to be worried. It's gonna be a little crazy, but you are not in danger. My bear would protect you even if you were. Okay?"

Lex said, "I wouldn't be here if I didn't trust you."

I kissed her quickly and stepped back a few feet and without another word shifted. She gasped as I came down on all fours as my bear. I didn't smell the scent of fear which made me happy. Once it was apparent she wasn't going to go running off into the woods screaming I stepped closer to her. She raised a hand and ran it across my snout and through my fur. As her hands petted me, I was more at peace than I ever had before in my life.

"You are gorgeous," she said, scratching me behind the ears.

Grizz, still in human form, walked over. "Sting. We're about to start."

He turned away from us and shifted. I walked Lex back to the fire. She sat next to Kim and rubbed the fur on my jaw.

"Have a good run," she whispered.

My heart was full to bursting when I turned away and bounded off behind the others into the woods for the run. I let out a roar of happiness as we ran.

Chapter 13 - Alexis

My breath came in short quick gasps, like I might be in shock. The good kind. Kim was next to me laughing. I shook my head and a smile spread across my lips as I watched the shifters galloping into the forest.

Kim said, "Yeah, it's pretty crazy the first time you see it. Like, damn, that guy just turned into a bear?"

I nodded absently, sitting down at the fire with the rest of the ladies. There was a young woman across from me that I recognized. Her name was Misty and she owned a cute little coffee shop, bookstore combo downtown.

Trying to get my mind off how surprised I was I spoke to her. "When was your first time? Seeing it I mean. Are you with one of the guys? Your boyfriend?"

Misty shook her head but gave me a big smile. "No, I'm here with a friend. One of the shifters named Rogue. I've known him for years, he's like my big brother. I come to these things every now and then to get out of the house. But, I will say, the first time I watched Rogue shift? I think I almost pissed myself."

The ladies all laughed. I liked this girl already. We sat around talking and after a half hour Kim said we all needed to get together one weekend.

"Do we want to go to Sting's place?" I offered.

Misty's eyes lit up. "Oh. I haven't been there yet. I've been so busy I haven't really had a night to myself. I've heard it's *the* place to be though. Let's do it."

We agreed about the time the men came pelting out of the forest, back to their normal human selves again. If anything, they look more wild and hopped up on energy than when they left. A few of them ran out still as bears.

"One warning, the guys are always revving to go after a run," Kim commented.

"Yeah, they are," a woman I didn't know said in a suggestive voice.

I looked at Kim in surprise. "You mean...?"

Kim didn't giggle. She laughed so hard she was slapping her leg. "Girl, just you wait. It's the most primal...Ugh. I don't even have words."

"It's hot as fuck," the same woman said. "The best sex of my life, hands down."

This was proven true a few seconds later as Hutch came running up, shifting back to human as he came upon our fire. His clothes, thanks to whatever shifter magic made it so, looked perfectly pressed, while he looked wild and out of control. He grabbed Kim, who squealed a laugh, picked her up and threw her over his shoulder and started walking toward the clubhouse. My jaw hung open as Kim looked at me over Hutch's shoulder and shrugged then smiled.

Rogue jogged up next and sat down next to Misty. He looked worked up and buzzed, but didn't look to be in the mood to take anyone to bed. He grabbed a beer out of a cooler beside the fire and downed it in two quick gulps, he belched and looked embarrassed. Misty laughed and he seemed to be a little less self-conscious.

Sting came over next, huffing breath and a sheen of sweat across his body. He looked amazing, and my body reacted. My body grew warm, and there was a bit of a twinge between my legs, watching him stride toward me. For an instant I thought, and maybe at the back of my mind hoped, he would scoop me up and carry me off like Hutch did to Kim. Instead he sat down next to me and pulled me close. I slid into his side and nestled against him, feeling the heat of his body. He smelled musky, but not in a bad way, it was a smell like nature, like the earth.

"Are you having a good time?" he asked, his voice somewhat husky.

"I am, actually. It's...well, it's something to see." I was a little disappointed that he didn't seem to crave me physically the way the others seemed to crave their women, but I kept that thought to myself.

We sat chatting with Rogue and Misty for a few minutes when he whispered in my ear. "You wanna go for a walk?"

"Yes. I need to stretch my legs."

I followed him into the woods, onto a well worn path. Once we were away from the bonfires things grew much quieter. I felt like I could ask some more personal questions, that I wasn't comfortable asking in front of everyone.

"What's it really like being a shifter? Does it ever get...annoying, or burdensome? I mean they make you live outside the city and stuff."

He thought a moment before he answered. "Well, there were times when I was growing up that I wished I'd been able to play with the other kids. I got over that pretty soon though. The pack is really close. I had all the family I ever needed here with them."

That made sense to me. "I wish I had something like that. Some support system to fall back on. I hate being part of my family because of how they treat me."

Sting stopped walking and turned me toward him. "Alexis, you are amazing. Your family is foolish for not seeing it. You make me feel like I can do anything. You're kind, you're smart, you're beautiful, I can't tell you how lucky I was when you said you would be my girlfriend."

Hearing him say all the things I always wanted someone to say made my heart skip. All the things

I'd told myself weren't true, that I had talked myself into believing weren't true. It left me vulnerable, and a little scared.

I bit back tears. "Nobody has ever said those things about me before."

"I'll remind you every single damn day how awesome you are. How fantastic you are if that's what you need to feel like you are the person I see."

Then, without waiting for my response he wrapped me in his arms and kissed me. I melted into him, letting Sting take me, his passion was like a flame that lit me on fire too. I wrapped my arms around him and kissed him back just as hard. He grew hard, pressing into my thigh. I gasped as his hands slid up and he clutched at my breasts through my shirt. I moaned into his mouth as he slid his thumbs across my nipples. Then his hands were down my back palming my ass. Before I wanted him too he pulled away gasping.

"Sorry, I need to calm down."

"I don't want you to," I murmured, initiating another kiss. He growled as I did it and I became wet hearing him.

Pulling away again Sting grinned. "If we keep this up I won't be able to stop myself from taking you home."

Feeling the warm throb between my legs, and the rush of being with him, it was exactly what I wanted. In fact, I would have been fine if he had me right there on the forest floor.

I looked him dead in the eyes and said, "Take me home."

He stared at me, the look of surprise shifting to an overwhelming lust as he leaned in and gave me another fiery kiss. He didn't say another word as he lifted me up and began speed walking up the path to his place. Nervous excitement melded with desire as I anticipated what would happen when we got there.

Chapter 14 - Sting

Bursting through the door of my place, I kicked it shut behind us. I wanted her so bad I could fucking taste it. My entire body vibrated with need. I put her down and pressed her against the door, making out with her again. Our lips intertwined and her tongue slipped into my mouth and made my dick so hard it was painful in my pants. All I wanted to do was reach down and pull myself out.

Backing away, gasping. "Are you sure this is what you want?" I asked.

Without a word, Alexis stared into my eyes and slid a hand down my stomach, cupping my crotch, squeezing gently. It was all I needed, she couldn't have been more direct. I lifted her into my arms again, she giggled as I ran upstairs. I threw her onto my bed and pulled my shirt over my head. I stared at her as I unbuttoned my pants, and she unbuttoned her dress. By the time I had my shoes and pants off Alexis was sitting on the bed in nothing but a bra and panties. My eyes ranged across her body, I grew harder seeing her like that.

She bit her lip and reached behind her, a moment later she pulled her bra free. Her breasts free, a growl of lust escaped my lips. Her caramel skin and dark nipples were the last straw. I jumped onto the bed and kissed her again, letting my hands slide down to her breasts. Her nipples were hard and erect beneath my fingers. I pinched them, a tiny bit of pressure, and she gasped.

"Does that feel good?" I whispered.

She nodded. "Uh huh, yeah," she said, her voice husky with desire.

I leaned down and took her breast in my mouth, flicking my tongue around the nipple. Her back arched, and her hands ran through my hair pulling me closer.

She whispered, "You've got to fuck me. I need it. I need you in me."

I slid my underwear off and rummaged in my bedside table for a condom.

"I'm on the pill, it's okay. It's fine, do it, please," she said while reaching a hand forward to grab and stroke my dick. It would be so much hotter without anything between us.

I groaned and let her work for a few seconds. Before I did anything else she rolled toward me and took me in her mouth.

"Oh fuck." I moaned watching her lips wrap around me.

She slid her mouth up and down, wet, slick, and fucking amazing. She sucked at me, her hand sliding down to caress my balls. I reached between her legs and slid a finger into her as she worked at me. She groaned as I moved the finger in and out of her. The faster I moved my hand the harder and faster she sucked at me. Finally I pulled out of her mouth.

"You're gonna make me cum," I said, dazed.

"That was the plan," she whispered, kissing my stomach.

"Not yet." I laughed and rolled her onto her stomach.

Her ass in the air I knelt and slid my tongue across her clit, into her pussy, then up to her ass and back down. I did it for several seconds before burying my tongue deep inside her, flicking it up and down, back and forth. I bit her gently in the lower back and butt. Then went back to working

my tongue between her legs.

"Jesus Christ fuck me already. Dear god."

That was all I needed to hear. After her saying

that, there wasn't a force on earth who could stop

me. Except Alexis herself, of course. Without

another word I lifted my face and entered her,

fast and deep, and Alexis shuddered under me,

cumming already. My desire, and the desire of my

bear made the next several minutes like a dream.

I slammed into her from behind, over and over.

Sweat poured from me, as I reached around her

and rubbed her clit as I thrusted. Lex was nearly

screaming as she came again and again.

It was building inside me, an explosion ready to burst. I'd never felt anything like this before. It was like my first time again. I was almost out of my mind when it happened. I thrust into her and groaned so loud my throat hurt. I came for an eternity. I almost bit her then, almost marked her, but I buried my teeth against my own forearm. I collapsed beside her sweaty and spent.

We both lay there gasping when Lex finally said, "Holy fucking shit."

"Uh...yeah...same," I murmured with a smile.

She rolled onto her back and looked down at her naked body. I glanced over and saw I'd left a hickey and a couple bite marks on her breasts. It was embarrassing seeing them, but Lex smiled, laid her head back down and ran her fingers across the marks. My possessiveness over her grew even stronger, seeing that she enjoyed being marked by me.

I still apologized. "Sorry. I got...a little out of control."

She opened her eyes. "It's fine. Don't worry." She looked demure. "I kind of liked it."

I smiled. "Well, I liked all of it. I've, never in my life, had sex that good. Ever."

She reached over and stroked my chest. "Uh...yeah...same," We both laughed at her tease.

"Do you want to stay the night?" I asked.

"That would be great. Mostly because I don't think I can walk, much less drive home."

After getting ready and laying down we both fell fast asleep almost instantly. It was the best night's sleep I could ever remember, laying there with Alexis in my arms.

I woke up the next morning, still groggy. I rolled over and stretched a hand out for Lex. She wasn't there. I sat up, looking around. She wasn't in my room. A sudden sinking filled my chest. Had last night been too intense for her after all? Did she leave? Then I heard her laughing, from downstairs.

I stood up and went closer to the door. She was laughing and talking to someone. Who the hell was downstairs in my house this early? On a Saturday no less? I leaned close to the door to get a better listen. When Lex stopped laughing I finally recognized who was with her. My mother.

"Awe shit." I stumbled around the room grabbing clothes and trying to hurry downstairs as fast as my feet would allow. I needed to get down there before Mom could tell any embarrassing stories.

I came downstairs, and found Mom and Lex standing in the kitchen. Lex was fully dressed and you couldn't tell she'd been ravaged the night before. Except for the hickey on her neck, which was plainly visible.

"Hey Sweetie. I was coming by to drop off some leftovers from last night. Though, if I'd known you had company I would have brought more."

I stepped forward and took the container from her. "Thanks for thinking about me." And gave her a kiss on the cheek, I mumbled into her ear. "You could have called ahead."

She wrapped me in a hug and whispered back to me. "I didn't think I needed to. Never seen another woman in your house."

She was right. I never brought any of the girls to my house to hook up. That was something that only happened at the clubhouse. This was no hookup, she was mine. I was hers and she was mine? Was that real? I'd never had anything more than a casual relationship, and the realization I finally had more was pretty crazy.

Mom went and gave Lex a hug. "I need to get going, but I hope I get to talk to you more young lady."

"Thanks for the food Mom." I gave her another hug, and a kiss on the cheek as she made her way to the door.

"Bye." With that Mom went out and closed the door behind her.

"She's a sweet lady. I like her," Lex said.

I grabbed Lex and kissed her, hard, right there in the kitchen. I wanted to express how badly I wanted her, not only physically. I tried to make her feel that through the kiss.

"Wow, what was that for?" she asked as I pulled away.

"I liked seeing you in the kitchen with my mom."

She grinned and blushed. She looked gorgeous. I lifted the lid on what Mom had brought. It looked like roasted chicken and vegetables. Not really breakfast fare.

"You wanna go out for breakfast?"

"Oh sure. I met Rogue's friend Misty last night, we could go to her place. A little coffee shop in town."

I agreed and fifteen minutes later we were stepping through the door of the coffee shop.

Misty glanced up and saw us, a smile bright on her face.

"Oh my gosh guys. Glad you could stop by."

I nodded and waved. Lex stepped up the counter and started talking about a girls night they had planned the evening before.

"Are we still on for going to your new place?" Misty asked, nodding toward me.

"Yeah," Lex responded.

I didn't even try to hide the grin. I'd been letting Owen run things nearly every night now, so I wouldn't be there to intrude on their night out. It did make me happy that Lex wanted to be close to me and take her friends out to my club.

Misty helped us with our coffee and pastry orders, and we took a seat at a table outside on the sidewalk.

Lex said, "Okay, so--"

"Uh oh. Are we having *the talk*?" I asked, laughing.

She blinked and smiled. "How could you tell that?"

"Only serious conversations start with 'Okay, so', that's how."

She rolled her eyes. "Ugh, fine. Yes, let's have it then."

I took a bite out of my muffin and said, "Cool, I'll go first. Where do we stand now? After last night?"

She sipped at her coffee and said, "Well, I feel safe with you. I want to be with you. What are your long term *wants* for lack of a better word?"

"If I'm going to be with someone, I want commitment. I want someone who's as invested as I am. A partnership sort of."

Nodding, she said, "Same here. After the life I've had...." She trailed off and thought for a moment, then finished. "I want love eventually."

I took her hand in mine. "I can tell you that, in the few weeks I've known you, you deserve love more than anyone I've ever met. If you stick with me kid? You'll end up with more than you could ever want."

I smiled watching her blush and glance away shyly. We sat for a minute or two enjoying each other's company, thinking about what to ask next. The next question came from Lex, and I'd already anticipated it.

"I do know that I want kids one day. I know that's not probably in the cards if we stay together right?"

I chewed at my lip before I said, "Well, the odds aren't great, but it isn't zero. As Grizz and Zoey found out. That's a bridge we can cross over when we come to it."

We talked for a few more minutes about anything and everything that might come up in the days and weeks ahead. Misty came out at one point and brought us to-go cups of coffee 'on the house'.

Right before we were ready to leave Lex touched my arm and asked, "I want to be sure I'm totally clear on this. We are officially dating right?"

The only answer I gave her was leaning across the table and kissing her. I let my lips linger on hers for a long time, making sure that if anyone walked by they would know this was my lady. I moved back and looked her in the eyes and smiled.

Lex smiled back and replied. "Okay then. That's settled."

Chapter 15 - Alexis

My phone buzzed again. I stood up, I'd been helping one of the kids with their letters and numbers. I knew who the text was from. I glanced at Kim and nodded at the screen. She understood and came over to take my place.

I slipped into the break room and pulled my phone out. It was what I'd expected. My mother and sister again. I'd blocked their numbers, but they had both purchased burners at Walmart or something. I hadn't had the mental energy to block the new numbers. The first few texts hadn't been as nasty or vitriolic, so I'd let them come. I'd still ignored them, but I'd let the two of them get it all off their chest. That hadn't lasted long though.

The last two days they'd been inundating me asking me if I was coming to the bridal luncheon. It was probably themed to be a fucking princess tea party knowing Bridget. I informed them that I had not planned to attend that either. They'd responded as I was sure they would. I was ruining Bridget's wedding, I was not thinking of others, I was going to get disowned, how I was purposely hurting my sister. The last one was a crock of shit since they both purposely hurt me all the time.

I glanced through the messages, not bothering to read them all. I finally sighed and blocked both numbers. I vowed I'd block any new numbers they got too. I sat at the break room table and took a deep breath. It felt liberating, and I liked it.

Sting had been texting me throughout the day. I'd let him know about the messages from my family, and he'd been checking up to make sure I was good. Once I was back home, he finally called me that night to see how I was.

"Hey there. How did the rest of the day go with the two battle axes?"

"Ugh, I finally blocked them. I'd had enough of their shit. I'll block them again if they get new phones."

Sting said, "That's probably for the best. Forget them. I know how toxic families can be."

I frowned and realized I still hadn't asked why he and his Mom had moved to Forest Heights in the first place all those years ago.

"Sting, what did your Dad do to you guys?"

I was worried I'd pushed too far. Maybe I'd dug into a sore spot he didn't want to explore, but he told me almost without hesitation.

"Pretty cliché, really. Abusive father smacks around his wife and kid. Wife and kid take off. I really don't have one good memory of him. Some of the other guys in the crew had shit Dads, but they could at least think of something good. 'My Dad's a drunk, but he always took me to ball games', 'my dad ran around on my mom, but he always made me laugh when I was scared', shit like that. Not me though. One of the happiest days of my life was the day Mom packed me and what we could carry into the car and ran for Forest Heights. My aunt was in the Clan back when Grizz's Dad ran it. He helped shelter us from my dad. I know it should go deeper, but that's pretty much the whole story."

"Oh geez," I said, feeling thankful that at least Mom wasn't physically abusive on top of everything else. The emotional abuse had been bad enough. "Have you seen him since you guys left?"

"Nope. Haven't even talked to him. But the last few months he's been reaching out. Mom really wants me to sit down with him. I don't know why. I think she's hoping there will be some kind of eye opening, angels singing, rainbow lit reconciliation if I just have lunch with the old fuck. Not gonna happen though."

"I get that, yeah. It's your decision, even if your Mom wants it, it's still your life."

Sting cleared his throat and changed the subject. "Anyway, I wanted to tell you about your girl's night outing this weekend."

"Oh yeah?"

"Yeah. I did a little something special. I booked you guys a private table at the place. Owen will be looking for you and he'll get you all set up. Also, and this is me working on brownie points for the moment I inevitably screw up down the road, I hired a private driver to pick you guys up and take you home. That way you can enjoy yourselves."

My jaw fell open. "Sting. Seriously? First, there's nothing saying you're going to screw up. So far you're… well, you didn't have to do that, but it'll be awesome anyway. Thanks, babe." I'd been about to tell him he'd been perfect, but that seemed like a bit much.

I heard the smile in his voice when he spoke next. "It's the least I can do for my lady. I won't be there that night. I don't want to be one of *those* boyfriends. You know the kind, won't let their woman out and about by themselves. But I am only a call away. I can get to the lounge in like ten or fifteen minutes max, remember that."

Butterflies swirled in my stomach. I liked Sting a lot. More than anyone I'd ever dated, and him doing this made me like him more.

"I'll let you go Lex, gotta get some dinner in me."

I wanted to tell him I wanted something in me too, but didn't have the guts to do it over the phone.

"Yeah, me too. See you soon."

The rest of the week I found that my mom and sister had discovered new ways of shaming me. Social media was a fucking cancer on the world. They posted about me, which made the rest of my extended family talk about how ungrateful I was. they'd tried messaging me through the apps as well, but I deleted them without reading. By Friday morning I'd blocked almost everyone I was related to. It hurt to do that. It also hurt to see some people in my family take my mom and sister's words to heart without asking me what was going on. Cousins, aunts, uncles? Many of them I liked. I'd finally had enough and called my dad.

After explaining everything that had happened all week he sounded tired and angry.

"Baby, I'm sorry. I don't get on those apps, I didn't have any idea they were doing that. I'll get to the bottom of this. I'll handle it. This is not okay behavior."

I had tears in my eyes when I said, "Thank you Daddy. I love you."

"Love you too."

I hung up feeling a little better. At least someone was in my corner other than Sting. After dealing with all this the whole week I was more than ready for tonight. I needed to let off some steam. I had plans to get pretty hammered and forget all about this shit for a night.

Kim and Misty arrived at my place at seven. Misty and I stood at my kitchen table and knocked back two shots each, pregaming before the club. Kim didn't drink but she was happy to watch us get wasted. The car got there about fifteen minutes later. It was a massive glossy black SUV. The driver was dressed in a black suit and got out to open our doors for us. Inside sat a bucket filled with ice and a bottle of champagne for Misty and I, and a bottle of sparkling grape juice for Kim.

"Damn," Misty said as she got in beside me.

"Perks of dating the owner I guess." I shrugged.

We got to the lounge and Owen was waiting for us at the door, and escorted us to the

VIP section table Sting had promised. He then handed us menus.

"Custom menus prepared for the ladies by the Chef at our Proprietor's request," Owen said as he handed them around. "On the house, of course," he finished with a smile.

Kim sighed and laughed. "Okay, that's it. Hutch is opening a place too. That or he's coming to work for Sting. I need these perks in my life."

We ordered more drinks and ordered our food, most of which were words none of us understood. I had to Google what foie gras was. After that we relaxed and enjoyed the music.

"So, how's it going with Sting?" Misty asked.

I moaned. "Too good. Not good enough. I don't know. It's hard to trust something like this."

"Sting is a great guy," Misty said. "You're lucky."

I sighed and tried changing the subject. We discussed our weeks, I left out my family drama, and eventually Kim and I asked Misty about any guys she might be dating.

She finished off her martini and said, "Well, not right now. I had a couple guys last year that I dated for a while, but it didn't stick. If I'm honest I wish Rogue would ask me out."

Kim's eyebrows went up. "Oh shit. You have the hots for Rogue?"

Misty grinned humorlessly. "A little yeah. We've been friends for years. He's super sweet, but has made it *very* clear he doesn't want to date humans. He's such a good friend I don't want to screw that up by pushing something that obviously isn't going to happen."

Misty looked pretty sad about the whole thing, my heart for her seeing the dejected look she had when she spoke about it. It was sweet that she wanted to keep their friendship intact.

Kim said, "Look, the best thing you can do is find a guy who does want to be with you. It sounds like waiting around for Rogue is a lost cause. You shouldn't be alone pining away from some dude."

Misty perked up and laughed. "You're right."

"Me and Lex will be your wingmen, no fuck that, wingwomen. If you find someone you like let us know.

It was a great plan in theory, but by the end of the night Misty and I were pretty wasted. Instead of being a wingwoman, Kim turned into a babysitter. We were too hammered to even think about men. It didn't stop them from approaching us though. They all got turned down. Most were cool about it, while others called us bitches for rejecting them, but we laughed and shrugged that off.

I sent Sting a few drunk texts throughout the night. They got more ridiculous the more drinks I had. One was a pretty vivid written description of what I wanted to do to him the next time I had him naked. He sent back multiple laughing face emojis. I really wanted to see him, but I told myself not to be the clingy girl who can't even have a night out without seeing her boyfriend.

I barely remembered the ride back home in the SUV. We got back to my place and inside without incident. I chugged water trying to sober up a little bit before bed, Misty did the same. Kim still had to help me find pajamas...in my own house. She took Misty to the guest room where she got her into bed, Kim told me she was going to take the futon in there to make sure Misty was good the rest of the night.

I went back to my room and took a quick shower, which did help clear my head a little. I put my pajamas on and was pulling the covers down on my bed when my phone buzzed. It was a text from Sting.

Sting: come to the door

What the hell? I thought. I went to the front door and opened it. Sting stood there, and looked good enough to eat. Before I even spoke he growled and slid forward, taking me in his arms and kissing me in that way he had that always took my breath away. When he broke away it was like I was getting drunk all over again.

He ran a hand down my back and clutched my butt. "Tomorrow night? You're mine."

He smiled and gave me a quick kiss before turning and walking back to his bike. I stood there, lightheaded. I closed and locked the door as he pulled away. I crawled into bed, and tried not to dream about what tomorrow night might entail. If I did, I might not fall asleep for some time. I finally dozed off with a smile on my lips.

Chapter 16 - Sting

Mom wouldn't quit calling or texting me since meeting Lex. I knew it would just keep on, until I saw her. I made the trip up to her house Saturday morning. She was waiting with a tray of bacon, egg and cheese biscuits. One thing about Mom, I never left hungry. I hugged her and sat on the porch with her eating breakfast.

After a bite I said, "I guess you want to know about Lex?"

"I didn't say that, but I would like to know more about this sweet lady I found in your kitchen the other day."

Rolling my eyes, I bit back a sarcastic retort. "And the half dozen calls and texts checking in on me? You weren't fishing for information?"

She put her biscuit sandwich down and grabbed a glass of orange juice. "Well, fine then. You've seen through my poorly disguised ruse. Now. Spill it mister."

I laughed and finished my breakfast before starting in on the story. I told Mom everything, from the moment I met her, to the moment we decided to officially be a couple. I, of course, left out the triple X portions. I was very close to my mom...but not that close.

"It all sounds like something out of a story book Reese. My boy? The grand hero saving the damsel from her evil family? Oh, I should write a book."

"Please don't."

"Well, I'm happy for you sweetie. I support you, and only want the best for you."

Her words were uplifting and happy, but she looked bothered by something. I had a hunch, and I was not in the mood for it.

"Thanks, Mom. I appreciate it. Can you tell me what else is bothering you?"

She stared at the floorboards of the porch and shook her head. "It's still your father. I've been talking to him, even though you told me not to."

"Son of a bitch. Mom, I told you I don't want to talk about this. I don't want you getting mixed back up with him either."

"Reese, hear me out. I promise you this is not me trying to get back with your father. That will never happen, trust me. It's just that I am the one link he has to his son, to you. He wants to know how his son is."

I slapped my hand on the armrest of the chair. "He doesn't get to know. He doesn't deserve to know about me or what I'm doing. And you need to end this shit once and for all."

Her face was pained, and her hands twisted in knots in her lap. "I want us all to heal, to have some closure."

I laughed without humor. "You all don't get it. I have done my healing, I don't need anymore closure. This seems like it's more about you two than it is about me. For the very last time. I don't want anything to do with my old man. That's final, and I'm not saying it again. I love you Mom, but I gotta go."

"Reese, wait."

I ignored her and stomped down the porch and got on my bike and pulled away. It was shitty leaving that way, but I'd had enough. I'd said for months I didn't want to talk to him. After a while you get pissed when people don't want to listen to what you're saying.

The rest of the morning I was in a crappy mood. I needed to try to get over it before my date that night with Lex. I headed to the clubhouse, hoping for a game of pool or something to get my mind off it. When I walked in, Rogue was sitting at the bar. He looked confused and frowning.

"Hey man, what's up?"

He glanced up and nodded to me. "Oh nothing. Just...something weird happened."

I pulled up a stool next to him. "Do tell. I like weird."

"Well, Misty called me to let me know she was going out on a date."

"This is weird how?"

"We never really talk about dating and who we're going out with. It's kind of strange. Then, when I said to be safe, she got kind of upset and irritated with me. I don't get it."

Biting my lip I wondered if my friend could really be as dense as he seemed to be. It was incredibly obvious that Misty had feelings for Rogue that went beyond friendship. It wasn't my place to point this out though. After a few minutes thinking Rogue shrugged.

"She must have been having a bad day."

I stared at him and shook my head. Things could be worse, I could be as blind as Rogue, fully oblivious to what was happening. Suddenly my problems seemed a little less complex. Rogue and

I talked a bit and then I left to get ready for my date with Lex.

The trip was for me to spend time with Lex, but it was also for business purposes. I wanted to source some new wine for the lounge, so I was taking her up to a winery for an overnight trip. I picked her up at her place at two and we made the two hour drive to the winery. We spent the drive enjoying each other's company. We were still in the getting-to-know-you phase of the relationship and we talked about all the random things new couples go over. Favorite elementary school teacher, favorite cartoon as a kid, if you were stuck on a desert island what's the one snack you would ask for. Mine was peanut butter cups, hers was licorice whips.

"Oh fuck. Seriously?"

She laughed. "What? They're delicious."

I made a comic gagging sound. "You better be glad you're sexy, smart, and funny, because otherwise I'd have to reevaluate our relationship after that answer."

She made a mock shocked face and swatted me on the arm. "Oh, and peanut butter cups is such a better answer? I didn't know you were a basic white chick."

"Well now you know. I like trashy tv and home renovation shows too."

We got to the winery at just after three, and went for a tour of the facility and the fields first. They then brought us up to a tasting room that overlooked the fermentation area on one side, and the vineyard fields on the other. The owner knew I was here as a possible customer so he brought out about a dozen bottles for us to sample.

I thanked him then spoke to Lex. "I know you guys got pretty wild last night, so make sure we pace ourselves."

Lex rolled her eyes at me. "We didn't get that plastered."

I leaned forward and raised my eyebrows. "I saw the bar tab. I know exactly how hammered you guys got."

She chuckled. "Okay, mister boss man, maybe we had some fun. I only plan on having a sip of each. You can drink as much as you want, then I can take advantage of you."

I laughed and popped the cork on the first wine. "Promises, promises."

Stopping, I stared at her with ideas of what he might do to take advantage running through my mind.

Lex sensed my mood... something in the air, the way I was looking at her, maybe. She held her glass and stared at my lips, and it was all I could do not to lean forward and capture her mouth with mine.

Pulling back, I cleared my thrat and poured our glasses from the first bottle.

This was going to be a difficult night.

By the sixth bottle Lex had been true to her word by only having a few sips of each. She helped me write notes on which wines were best, and which to mark off the list. Even drinking that little bit Lex was getting pretty giggly by the time we were done. The owner came back around and I ordered three cases of each of the ones we liked.

"Is our table ready?" I asked.

"Indeed it is Mister Kelly."

Lex frowned. "Our table?"

I took her by the arm and walked her to the stairs leading away from the tasting room.

"They have a five star restaurant here too. I figured it would be easier to have dinner in the same place," I said.

"Oh." She leaned in and whispered, "Are you trying to get lucky tonight?"

My hand drifted down and I squeezed her butt. "Maybe."

We rounded a corner and came to the maitre d of the restaurant.

"Mister Kelly? Miss King? Your table is this way, follow me please."

We walked through the dinning room to the back where a table was set with lit candles.

"Fancy," Lex whispered to me. "I didn't think you were the romantic type."

I picked up the menu. "Oh, just wait. You ain't seen nothing yet."

After what had to be one of the best meals of my life, we made our way to the hotel. There was a nice little boutique hotel near the vineyard. We checked in and headed up to our room.

Before I unlocked the door I looked at her and smiled. "I told you I was romantic."

I unlocked and opened the door. Stepping inside she could see the room had been set up like something from a movie. I'd called ahead to have it made perfect. Rose petals were scattered across the bed and in a trail leading to a hot tub. There was a bucket with a bottle of champagne beside the bed, and the entire room was lit with candles. I grinned watching Lex's reaction. She was a little tipsy and was more emotional than she probably would have been.

There were tears in her eyes when she turned to me. "No one has ever done anything like this for me before."

I slid a hand up and cupped her cheek. "As long as you're mine I'll always do my best to make you feel special. Because you are."

She pulled me into a kiss, then said, "Thank you so much. It really has been an amazing night."

I brushed a strand of hair from her face. "It's not over yet."

Chapter 17 - Alexis

Sting poured me a glass of champagne then turned the jets on in the hot tub on. I was relaxed, but not tired, I was anything but tired. My heart ached seeing how much trouble he'd gone to to make this night perfect. I was like I'd really found someone who would take care of me, and it was good. It had been such a long time, seeming to just be floating along on my own. Waiting.

Sting started disrobing and I sipped at my drink, watching him. He unbuttoned his shirt and slid it off. His abs rippled as he twisted to lay the shirt on the dresser. I bit my lip, thinking of what he was about to do to me. Shit, what I was about to do to him. There was a pleasant little twinge between my legs already. I downed the rest of the glass and unzipped my dress and let it fall to the floor.

Sting glanced at me and stared into my eyes and I slipped off my bra and slid my thong down to the ground. He kept his eyes locked on mine as I stepped over the tub and slowly got in. The fact that his eyes never left mine, never glanced down at my naked body, was erotic. It was like he was really looking at *me*. All of *me.* I was wet by the time I sat into the water.

"Come on big boy. Tit for tat," I whispered, nodding at his pants.

He grinned then unbuttoned and slid his pants down. Then he pulled his boxers down. I sighed pleasantly seeing his thick cock swing free and already imagined what it was going to do to me. I forced myself to not reach under the water and play with myself right then. He stepped forward and joined me in the hot tub.

Sliding over to him, I pressed my wet body to his, and kissed him deeply. He kissed me back and his hands found their way to my breasts. I moaned as his fingers found my nipples. My hand slipped under the water and took his cock in my hand, stroking it slowly. His body trembled with pleasure beneath me, and it was amazing to know that I was doing this to him. My fingers slid down and I caressed his balls while kissing and sucking at his neck.

With a growl he lifted me out of the water, and sat me on the edge of the tub. I sucked in a breath of surprise as he buried his face between my legs. I let out a long low groan and wrapped my legs around his head as he went to work on me. His tongue flicked across my clit, a finger slid inside me. The cool air and my moist skin had my nipples hard as rocks and aching pleasantly. I let him have his fun for several minutes, but I wanted to thank him for everything he'd done for me.

I pushed his head away, a pang of disappointment as his lips and tongue left me. I slid back into the water and kissed him again.

"My turn. Sit up," I whispered.

He obliged by sliding up out of the water onto the edge as I'd been. His dick stood erect and throbbing. I didn't hesitate, I slid my lips around it and took him as far as my mouth would allow. I pulled him in deep and sucked gently.

"Holy god." He gasped, and my pussy pulsed even more knowing I was pleasing him.

I slid my lips and mouth up and down, licking, sucking, and thrusting into him. He thrust his hips toward me, fucking my mouth gently as I moved. It was so sexy I almost came right then. When it seemed like he might be getting close he pulled his cock from my mouth, and sat back into the water.

Sting grabbed my ass, lifted me up and sat me down right on his cock. Being filled made my eyes roll back, he was so big I couldn't even speak as he started fucking me. Slow at first, deep and gentle thrusts while he sucked on my nipples. A delicious warmth spread from my pussy to the rest of my body.

I slid my fingers through his wet hair and took hold of him, staring deep into his eyes.

"Fuck me, babe. Do it, I want it."

He growled again and spun me around, my butt on the edge of the hot tub. He entered me and slammed himself into me. Harder and faster than before.

"Oh fuck. Yes. Just like that." I moaned.

"Is this what you want?" He grunted softly.

"Baby, give it to me. I love it."

A drunk grin spread across my face as he wrapped his hands around me, grabbing my breasts and the fucked me even harder. My body edged closer with every thrust. A dizzying throb pulsated through me. Sting gently pinched my nipples and thrust into me, deep and hard, and my body erupted.

"God." I shuddered and came, my core clenching over and over as the orgasm rolled through me, drying out my mouth and making my breath come in pants and bursts. The orgasms with Sting were unlike any I'd ever had, potent...overwhelming. I couldn't stop my moans and cries as Sting continued sliding into me over and over.

He seemed to go even faster after I came. I was panting for breath, hanging onto the side of the tub when another shuddering wave of pleasure swept over me. My nipples tingled, and my pussy throbbed. Each time he slammed into me again it was like my body shattered with pleasure.

I slipped a hand down and clutched his ass. "Baby, cum, please. I want to feel you cum."

Within seconds of me saying it his body trembled. "Fucking shit." He groaned, his face buried between my shoulder and neck.

His cock slid into me again and again, but slower now. He finally came to rest inside me, and placed his cheek against mine. He kissed me, and wrapped me in a hug.

"That was amazing," he whispered.

"It was. Let's go to bed," I said, and we both started laughing.

I woke up the next morning to Sting kissing me. I opened my eyes and saw that he was laying a tray across my lap. Breakfast in bed, pancakes, and sausage.

"You're spoiling me."

"You deserve to be spoiled."

I had the strange thought that this man was some mental creation I'd conjured. A hallucination of the perfect person for me. He seemed too good to be true. My mind was trying to tell me that soon the rug would be pulled out from under me and all this would come crashing down. Falling apart, just like with Tony.

No. I thought. *I don't need that negativity. This is nothing like with Tony. I didn't need to think about things like that because Sting is not Tony.* I didn't let the thoughts show on my face. I simply smiled and ate my breakfast, enjoying Sting's company.

A couple hours later we were checked out and walking through the lobby, rolling our overnight suitcases behind us. A voice rang out and shattered what had been one of the most pleasant twenty four hours of my life.

"How fucking dare you. I can't believe you have the nerve to be here."

I stopped dead in my tracks, the sound of Bridget's voice so incongruous that I thought I might still be in bed dreaming. I turned around and saw Bridget standing, her hands crossed angrily over her chest. The other five members of her bridal party stood around her, some looked at me with the same venom as Bridget, and some looked uncomfortable and embarrassed.

Of all the places for Bridget to be, this one was beyond unexpected I could't form words. I glanced over and Sting looked equally shocked and confused...and angry.

I finally managed a few words. "Why...Bridget, why are you here?"

My sister huffed and nodded to the girl beside her. "My Maid of Honor Holly thought a bachelorette trip to the vineyard would be a good way to wind down before the wedding. It would help calm my stress over my bitch of a sister dropping out."

Sting leapt forward a step and raised a finger. "That's your one shot. Choose your next words very fucking carefully."

His tone was like steel, there was no wiggle room, no space for negotiation, and Bridget looked taken aback and frightened. I was safe and protected with him here by me. I hadn't felt that way around my mom or sister for as long as I could remember. It made me more confident too, knowing he was there to stick up for me.

Bridget glared at Sting, but even she wasn't dumb enough to push him. Instead she turned her glare onto me. She slid her eyes up and down my body, then leaned back relaxing.

"You know what Lex? It's probably best if you aren't in the wedding party anymore. You're getting a little fat. You'd make the other girls look bad."

A couple of the girls chuckled, and Sting laughed. I tensed and looked at him. Was he agreeing with her? Was he laughing because I was fat?

Sting said, "Bridget it's ridiculous how jealous of Lex you are. You should have quit while you were ahead. Anyone with eyes can see Lex is the prettier one. That's why you always try to tear her down. You hate the fact that your sister not only got the brains, kindness, sweetness, and the personality, but she got the looks too. All you got was that shitty attitude from your bitch of a mother, and that fuggly ass face.

"She actually has a head on her shoulders, unlike you. She doesn't need to live off Daddy's money, unlike you. Bridget you don't have shit going for you, maybe you should humble yourself a little bit. You should be happy she won't be there for your wedding. You could walk in wearing a hundred thousand dollar dress and Lex could wear a paper bag, and she'd outshine the shit out of you."

Everyone, including me, was shocked by what he said. None of us, not even Bridget, could speak. Sting looked at me, his face stern and angry, but melting as our eyes locked.

"I meant every word of that," he said, wiping a tear from my face.

I hadn't realized I'd started crying. I felt stupid for it, but couldn't help it. I was so touched that I couldn't stop the tears if I wanted to. I collapsed into him, resting my head on his chest as he led me out the door into the parking lot. He kissed the top of my head, then opened the door and put me in.

The first few minutes on the drive home were quiet, but I finally worked up the ability to speak.

"Thank you. I've wanted to knock Bridget off her high horse for years. I just couldn't. I never was confident enough to say anything like what you did. What you said back there? It really meant the world to me. Thank you Sting."

He reached over and rubbed my shoulders. "I'll always have your back. But you need to start believing in yourself. You *are* better than her. You're better than your mother. You deserve respect, and you deserve to be treated well. Don't allow them to walk all over you. You are freaking amazing, and you need to start believing it."

I thought about that the entire trip home. It was good for me to hear someone say those things about me. Not only in the heat of the moment, but here, where no one else could hear. It wasn't for show, it was real.

We got home a few hours later and Sting walked me to my door. We had a long goodbye kiss at my door that I didn't want to end.

"Have a great week at work," Sting said. "Don't forget. You are fucking great. And I am lucky as hell you took a chance on me. I'm not going to squander that."

I stood on the porch and watched his truck

pull away. My mind was a complete jumbled mess

as I walked inside. All my emotions and thoughts

were spilling over each other. One thing was

ringing clear as a bell. I was falling in love with

that man.

Chapter 18 - Sting

Trey sat across from me going over the calendar of events for the next month. It was one of the jobs Owen and I had given him. It was surprising how organized Trey was.

He flipped the page. "Got a bachelor party booked for the weekend after next. The best man is riding my ass about letting them book a couple strippers, the answer is still no right? He's willing to add a grand to the rental cost."

I sighed and rolled my eyes. "Abso-fucking-lutley not. This is a classy place. Tell them I'll book them an SUV or limo to take them to a strip club afterward, but no tits and ass in my place."

Trey laughed. "I knew the answer, I just wanted to confirm."

When he pulled out another sheet, he got serious. "Got one I wanted to run by you too. Private party, not sure for what."

I put my phone down. "Sounds pretty tame, what's the big deal?"

He cleared his throat. "Name on the contract is Tony Givens."

I stared at him for several seconds letting the implications sift through my head. "You know who that is right?"

Trey nodded. "He has something to do with your new girl right? I've heard you cussing and saying his name. Thought you might want to cancel his contract. Give a refund."

I quickly gave Trey a run down on the whole family-wedding-ex drama. He leaned his head back and whistled after I was done.

"Okay so definitely refund the douchebag? He's clearly a dick. And the contract clearly states we reserve the right to refuse service."

"Yeah, but I'm a bigger man than that. Let him keep the rez. But talk with Owen, I want extra security here that night. Hire a couple guys from the gang too, shifters make great bouncers. No one wants to fuck with a guy who can turn into a

five hunded pound bear on a moments notice."

"How is it going with your new lady friend?"

Trey asked.

"That guy Tony? His loss was definitely my

gain. Can't remember being this happy."

Trey laughed. "You sound like a man in love

dude."

I chuckled at that, but I didn't deny it.

Instead I stayed quiet, because it was true. Each

day I was falling for Lex more and more. I really

hoped the feeling was mutual. Before I thought

about that anymore, the chime of the door

opening rang.

Without glancing up I called out. "Not open yet. Come back at seven."

"Lo' boy," the voice called.

I dropped my pen and my blood ran cold. My head slowly lifted and there standing by the door was my father. He'd aged since I'd last seen him, but it was obviously him. He looked good, one of the blessings of a shifter. I gritted my teeth.

"Trey, head to the back, help Owen with whatever he needs."

Trey, read the tension of the room, understood the situation and disappeared quickly. I stood and walked around the bar.

"Why the fuck are you here? Didn't Mom pass on the message? Or did you just fucking ignore it?"

"I've been trying to get a hold of you for months. Decided the phone wasn't working so I'd need to come in person."

"What the hell could be so damned important? No means no."

Dad looked down at his boots, took a deep breath, then looked me in the eyes and said, "You've got a little brother."

Of all the things that could have come out of his mouth that was probably the only thing that could have left me speechless.

"What are you on about?" I asked.

Dad pulled out a zippo lighter and fiddled with it, flicking it open and closed. "His name is Zachary. He's nine years old."

I barked a laugh. "Nine. Jesus Dad I'm almost thirty, that's a hell of an age gap between kids.

"Yeah, yeah. I know. I met his Mom from a different clan. Some stuff happened and I had another kid. What can I say, alright?"

I put my hands to the side of my head, shock and anger being pushed to the side in favor of confusion.

"What the fuck does this have to do with me?" I asked, still trying to get my head around the fact that I had a brother.

Dad sighed and snapped the lighter closed hard. "She's dead."

"You mean your baby mama?" I felt bad about being so flippant. As far as I knew she'd been a fine woman stuck with an asshole like Mom had been.

Without answering Dad said, "Car crash." Then going off subject he glanced around. "Do you really own this place? It's nice. Makes me proud."

I snapped. "Don't do that shit. Do not do that shit right now. The time to give me praise and kind words was around twenty-five years ago. Get back on target. Your lady died and left you with a kid. What does that have to do with me?"

"Reese—"

"Sting. Call me Sting, that's my clan name."

Dad appraised me and nodded. "Sting then. It's a strong name, I like it. Anyway, Sting, I'm not a good father. You know that."

I laughed. "Hello mister understatement."

He winced and went on. "I can't raise a kid by myself. I'm not made for it."

My guts twisted, knowing where this was going, but I could not fucking believe it. This piece of shit, who I hadn't seen or talked to in over twenty years was getting ready to ask me to raise his kid for him. Another kid he refused to take accountability for.

"I know Grizz Allen has a tight pack, really good guys. He's legendary, and you're pretty high up in that crew. Rumor had it you were opening up your own place too. It seemed like it might be best if Zachary came and lived with you."

"You mean you got lazy as fuck and got tired of being a Dad...again. So, you're dropping your problem off on me. Who the fuck do you think you are?" I was seething with anger, nearly trembling.

"Listen Ree...Sting, you're his family. I thought it would be better with you than dropping him off with some random pack. No real connection."

"Maybe that's something you should have thought about before knocking another chick up. They have these things called condoms right? Slip right on and prevent little *mistakes* from

happening."

All I wanted to do was to tell him to get the

fuck out. At the back of my mind, though, I

couldn't stop thinking of the kid. I remember how

miserable it was to live with my old man. The kid

was the same age I was when Dad decided having

a family was putting a cramp in his style. Before

he chose drinking and fucking over taking care of

his responsabilities. What would the kid's life be

like if Dad dropped him off someplace? He was my

brother too. If I'd learned anything being in the

Forest Heights crew and watching Grizz, Hutch,

and Trey, it was that family meant something.

Family was strong, I'd be damned if I let my old man drive another kid into the dirt.

"Fuck. Bring me the kid. Alright? I'll do it."

Dad visibly relaxed. "Thank you. Sting it really is for the best. I'll send money and what—"

"Shut the fuck up Dad. Listen to me." I looked him dead in the eyes. "If I'm going to take this kid to raise? I don't want you anywhere near either of us. Got it? It should be easy for you. You did it to me. You can do it to him."

I watched Dad grit his teeth, but the look on his face was sadness and dejection.

"Okay. Yeah, okay. I'll call you to meet up when it's time. Your Mom gave me your number."

"Cool, don't let the door hit you on the ass on the way out."

With that my father left the lounge. I stood, rooted in place, rage slowly boiling away. I was left with irritation and anger. Also fear. I wasn't in the greatest mood when Lex stopped by an hour later.

I was sitting at the bar going through emails and she stepped up and smiled at me.

"Hey there. How's your day going?" she asked.

I sighed, not taking my eyes off the screen. "It's...well it's fucking complicated."

"Sounds interesting."

I did my best not to take out any of my frustration on her, she didn't deserve it. But I wanted to blow up at someone, so I did my best not to snap at her. I guess I needed to let her know what was happening.

"I...uh...saw my dad today."

Lex's jaw dropped. "What?"

"Yeah he came by here to see me about an hour ago."

"Well what the hell did he want?"

"Oh you know the usual. Dropped a bomb on me. I apparently have a nine year old little brother, my dad's a prick and doesn't want him anymore, so he asked me to take him in and raise him. Just general stuff like that."

"What? Are you serious?"

I nodded, slamming the computer closed.

Lex asked, "Are you going to? Take him in that is?"

I laughed. "I don't think I really have a choice. His Mom died in a car crash a few months back and it was either that or the old man was going to leave him with the nearest shifter clan. I can't let the kid be abandoned like that. He's my brother for god's sake"

Lex leaned forward and took my hand. "I'll do whatever I can to help."

I came around the bar and took her in a hug. "I don't want to put that on you."

"You aren't putting it on me. The kid just lost his Mom, and his dad doesn't want him. He's going to need people around him that care. He needs people to love him. I can help do that. Christ, it's what I do for a living."

A lump formed in my throat and tears burned in my eyes. "I really don't deserve you. You know that right?"

She kissed me and said, "Maybe not, but you've got me anyway."

I smiled and pulled her close. The love for her was building every day. Like a pressure in my chest. I hoped I wouldn't be like my old man and fuck everything up.

Chapter 19 - Alexis

Several weeks had gone by and Sting was still dealing with all the legal wrangling that came along with taking custody of his brother Zachary. It was a lot more than any of us could've realized it would be.

He was insanely worried and stressed even though he was trying not to show it. Bless his heart. I didn't blame him. He wanted to do right by Zachary. He'd made a few trips out to his dad's clan to visit the boy.

When he came back, Sting hadn't said much other than that the child was quiet. Which Sting seemed to think was a result of both losing his mother and having to deal with the old man the last few months as his only caregiver. Apparently not a good thing.

I tried to help where I could, which included going out with Kim and Zoey to shop for things for Zachary's room. Zoey having Rainer made her the best bet on knowing what a boy that age might like. Thank goodness for friends. Having a clan like this was an amazing bond, even amongst the humans tied to the bears in one way or another.

Zoey's belly was getting nice and round. It was the beginning of October and she was probably a month or two away from delivery. She was a huge help and I was so thankful she agreed to come along, even as exhausted as she must've been.

We walked through the shopping center to a bookstore. I wanted to have a bunch of comic books, kid novels, and stuff in his room. Sting said he was quiet, so I wanted his room stocked with stuff he could do by himself until he warmed up to us and was able to interact better. Anything to make him feel safe and secure. And mostly, loved.

Kim asked, "So, Lex, what do you think about all this motherly stuff? Are you ready for that?"

I sighed, my heart hurting for the poor guy. "I'm not going to be his Mom. He had a Mom and lost her. That's not even something I'm entertaining the thought of. I almost want to learn along with him. It helps that I'm a teacher and I know how to nurture and give guidance. I can do that for him. I really only want to be a support system for Sting. He'll need help and he's already so busy and stressed, I need to take some of that off him."

Zoey glanced at Kim, and Kim smiled. I frowned and asked, "What?"

Zoey said, "Sweetie you sound like a woman in love."

I stared at them for a few seconds, instead of denying it I grinned and shrugged. Why bother protesting and all that? I wasn't in the mood to play games.

Kim and Zoey both gasped, then the questions started. When did I know? Do I think Sting feels the same? How do I feel? Have either of us said the magic words yet? I tried answering all the questions while we finished shopping, but they never seemed to end. Somehow, talking about it just made me grin rather than being annoying.

They both seemed happy for me. They did mention that they hoped I didn't have to deal with the same crazy shit they had to when they got with their respective shifters. After finding everything we needed I led them to the checkout area.

While checking out someone behind me spoke. "Alexis?"

My stomach fell, I knew that voice. I turned and saw Tony and Bridget standing off to the side. I was immediately on guard, but Kim stepped between them and me, giving a buffer.

Bridget crossed her arms and said, "Jesus Christ I hate how small this town is. It would be nice to go out anywhere and not run into my sister."

Finally, something we were on the same page about. "I couldn't agree more, Bridget. I'd love to not see you either." Ever.

Bridget looked shocked. She was used to jabbing at me, but she was not accustomed to me spitting them right back at her. I'd had enough though. I didn't care if it meant keeping the peace or not. I just wanted her out of my life.

She recovered quickly though. "Well, I won't be here long. We came to pick up some of our registry items for the wedding. It's been nice that at least *some* people can be supportive and help out. Honestly Lex, It's shocking how selfish you've been. I mean everything can't *always* be about you. Everyone can see your true colors now."

It made me irate that Bridget and Mom had made me out to be the bad guy. There wasn't anything I could do about it though. It was just something to live with. I had other things to think and worry about. My mother and sister's vindictiveness was not one of them. Having them out of my life would make it infinitely better.

"Well, Bridget, I hate that's how you are taking this. But I do hope the wedding goes well."

If I thought that would be the end of it I was wrong, Bridget can't help but throw another dig in.

"You know Lex, you might think you're hot shit with your trashy little shifter boyfriend, but it won't be long before he realizes you're a bore. He'll leave you high and dry for something better. Just like Tony did."

Before I said anything, Kim stepped forward. "You are such a bitch. Shut your mouth.

Everyone knows Tony is a fucking man whore who can't keep his dick in his pants, and he's being forced into a marriage he doesn't want. All because he's a pussy and can't admit he still has the hots for Lex and wants to get back with her."

Bridget shoved Tony. "Tell that bitch it's not true Tony. Tell them."

Tony glanced at me, and for a split second he looked at me the way he had back in highschool when we first got together. Like I'd hung the moon and painted the stars. It made my chest ache, I remembered how that look made my heart flutter. Now it just hurt like hell, knowing everything he'd done to me.

When Tony didn't answer Bridget's face went a livid red and she shoved him again, harder. "Tony. Goddammit. Tell them it isn't true."

He finally dropped his gaze from me and mumbled. "No, that's crazy. I don't care about her."

No one believed that, not even Bridget. She looked ready to murder Tony. Not wanting any part of it, I turned back and kept checking out. It must have been awful for the poor girl scanning our items. She'd seen the whole exchange, and looked like she wanted to be anywhere but right there. We paid and headed to the parking lot, all the while listening to Bridget and Tony have an intense whispered argument behind us.

I'd hoped that would be it, but Bridget followed us out the door and kept trying to goad me on.

"You know Daddy only treats you the way he does because he thinks you're pathetic. Fat, pathetic, and forever alone."

Kim leaned over to me and whispered, "Do you want me to punch a bitch? Because I have no qualms about throwing hands in this parking lot."

"Just ignore her. Let's get in the car and go," I said.

Zoey and Kim had me get in the car as they loaded up everything. I still heard Bridget trying to yell at us, but I tuned out the words. All I could really think about was what Kim had said and the way Tony looked at me. He was still harboring feelings for me. I didn't know what to think about that.

We got to Sting's place and set everything up in the room, getting ready for him. Sting arrived home a few minutes after Zoey and Kim left. He walked into Zachary's room and smiled while he walked around.

"It looks great. Thanks so much. This was a huge help." He grabbed me and hugged me. "I don't know how I would have done this without you."

It was good to be of help, I kissed him and said, "It was no trouble at all."

His smile faltered as he looked at me. "What's wrong? There's something on your mind, I can tell."

My mind spun and I tried to think of what I wanted to say, to talk about. But things were still jumbled and I didn't know where to start. After a second of two I decided it wasn't worth talking about. It was a silly moment of doubt, a *what might have been*, and that was it. I had no desire to think about Tony or what might've been. I knew what kind of man he was now. It certainly wasn't worth telling Sting about. Not when he was ten times the man Tony was. "Nothing, just a busy week. I'm tired."

Sting studied me a few more seconds before shrugging it off and looking at the room some more. I sighed inwardly, I did not want to dwell on the fact that I'd been a little glad that Tony still thought me. Knowing he might still want to be with me filled me with a strange longing. I didn't want him back, but my selfish side was happy knowing he was in an unhappy relationship and was probably miserable.

The fact that I was happy about someone being miserable was out of character for me. It made me question whether or not I was a bad person. It was strange and I didn't like it. I knew what I needed, but didn't want to admit it. I needed closure, and that meant I needed to talk

to Tony.

Chapter 20 - Sting

By the end of October I had every legal thing taken care of for me to take over as Zachary's guardian. I'd gone to visit him a couple times a week since all this started. The first few visits were really weird. Like, 'Hey, I'm the brother you didn't know you had, who's also old enough to be your Dad.' But after getting to know the kid things became easier. In fact after visiting him, it solidified the fact that I was making the right decision. He was quiet and withdrawn, who the hell wouldn't be after losing their Mom and living with my old man. Jesus, it sounded like a living hell. I was grateful to Lex for getting his room all set up, it would make the transition much easier.

The day Zachary moved in Lex wasn't there. She and the social worker thought having anyone other than me there might overwhelm the boy. The house had been inspected multiple times by the social worker. My house was on Shifter Compound grounds, but Zachary's Mom and Dad were both shifters so that was not something to be marked against me. In fact it helped the state decide that I would be a good fit, along with the fact that I was family and financially secure. I needed to thank Lex, Kim, and Zoey too. I'd been far too busy to get my house up to snuff and they'd spent countless hours cleaning and painting and anything else they could think of to help make a good impression.

The social worker pulled up in my driveway and my stomach gave a little jump when she got out with Zachary. He waved to me and walked up the steps. The social worker stayed back kind of in the shadows, watching but trying to not be obviously present.

"Well Zachary, this is the place. Kitchen is over there, we've got a lot of snacks and stuff in the pantry. Anytime you're hungry just ask, I'll take care of it."

"Cool." Was all he said. The kid was always quiet so I wasn't concerned.

"Living room, dining room, I usually eat at the kitchen bar, but we can do whatever."

"It's nice."

I nodded, Down the hall we got two bathrooms, one for me and one for you. So, you get your own."

"I've never had my own bathroom." There was a hint of emotion when he said that and I grinned.

"Also we have a huge clubhouse and stuff on the property. Pool tables, darts, video games, the whole nine yards. We can head there anytime you want. And once you are comfortable you can go up whenever you want to on your own."

He didn't say anything about that. He may

have had bad memories of Dad's clubhouse, so I

left it there. We walked down the hall and I hoped

he would like his room. It was my last ace in the

hole to get some emotion out of him.

"Here's your room," I said and opened the

door, stepping aside.

Zachary looked up and froze, his eyes slowly

widening, taking it in. There was a desk and chair

in the corner, a queen sized bed along the wall.

He'd been sleeping in a sleeping bag at my dad's

place. There was a huge bookshelf filled with

books, graphic novels, and comic books. Lex and

Zoey had decorated the walls with superhero

posters as well as Seattle Seahawk and Boise State

sports memorabilia.There was a thirty-two inch tv mounted on the wall with a streaming box attached, so he could watch what he wanted on Netflix, with parental controls installed of course. Finally there was a huge bean bag chair in the middle of the room.

He turned and looked at me. "This is all mine?"

"Sure is, bud," I said smiling.

Zachary's face shattered into a grin, and a few tears. "It's amazing. I love it."

I let out a deep breath not realizing I'd been holding it. "Glad you like it."

After a few check up questions from the social worker, she had me sign a couple more papers and then left. Once she was gone it felt a little awkward, until I asked Zachary if he wanted to go out for pizza?

"Pizza? I haven't had pizza in...a couple years I think."

Jesus Christ Dad? The simplest fucking meal and you couldn't be bothered to even do that?

"Saddle up big guy. It's pizza time. And you get to pick all the toppings you want."

The next few days with my brother were spent getting him acclimated to the new normal. He seemed pretty good, though, there were times when he seemed zoned out or lost in his own head. He'd had a tough time understanding why his dad was always gone, why his Mom always seemed sad. He'd probably seen the same abuse I'd seen as a kid, so I let him deal on his own without pressing. I gave him space since I was pretty much the only person who knew exactly where he was coming from.

Lex and I texted and called multiple times each day. It was a great break, getting a few moments to talk to her, and I missed her so much. She told me how great I was doing, encouraging me when I believed I was doing a shit job at something. I loved her so damned much, and needed to see her. It was just too soon to spring a new person on Zachary. I knew I needed to make time for Lex and me soon though, I was dying to see her.

There was a pack meet coming up the next Friday, and I thought that might be the best place to introduce Zachary and Lex.

I called Lex to ask her about it. "Hey," I said warmly. It was great hearing her voice.

"Hi," she said, her voice warm and happy. Damn, I made her sound like that. I wanted to wrap my arms around her and hold her all night.

And other things.

"There's a pack meet next Friday. I want to introduce you to Zachary."

She paused for a second, then sighed. "Oh, babe I can't make it, I'm sorry."

I was a little surprised. She didn't explain why, and I didn't push. I didn't expect an explanation. She was allowed to have a life that didn't revolve around the pack, but it wasn't like her to not be there.

My voice came out all disappointed, no matter how I tried to hide it. There was no way she didn't hear it. "Hey no big deal, next time though."

"Definitely."

I hung up and tried not to stew on it. Instead I worked on getting Zachary integrated into the pack. Zachary turned ten in November and that meant his first shift was quickly approaching. I wanted him to be comfortable with friends before his first shift. I would be on the lookout for symptoms for the next few months until it happened. By the night of the meet, I'd already talked to Grizz and Zoey about having Rainer there to maybe be a playmate.

Friday night Rainer was the first person to introduce himself to Zachary. I breathed a sigh of relief as it seemed the boys hit it off almost immediately. I stood off to the side with Grizz while Zachary and Rainer talked around the fire about the things boys talked about, superhero movies, Pokemon, terrible music. Then Rainer introduced Zachary to several other shifter kids.

Grizz nudged me and said, "The greatest gift I was ever given was my kids." He glanced over at Zoey who looked ready to pop.

"Now I know Zachary isn't your son, but he's going to look to you for guidance and help.

You should think hard and long about those moments and cherish them."

I nodded, understanding. I looked out at my little brother. He'd been through a lot lately. All wanted was the best for him. That thought process brought me back to Lex. She'd already healed me in so many ways, I hoped she could do the same for Zachary.

Grizz sidled up next to me and said, "Sting, there's nothing like the love of a good woman to make a man want to be better."

I smiled. "I can't agree more with you, Grizz."

The night was going great, but I still hadn't seen Rogue. Which was weird, I'd never seen him miss a meet. An hour or so in he finally showed.

He pulled up on his bike and got off looking kind

of mopey. His head hung low and kicked at rocks

as he came up the drive. He made a straight shot

for me.

"Sting, I need to talk to you."

I frowned, but checked to see that Zachary

was still playing with Rainer and some other kids,

so I pulled Rogue off closer to the woods out of

ear shot.

"What's up bro?" I asked.

Rogue sighed, and put his hands on his hips.

"Alright, I was able to hack Tony's phone

remotely, and get access to his social media

accounts. This dude had like two, maybe three

dozen messages written to Lex over the last year and a half. He never sent them, though. They're just sitting in his inbox. I also found a message chain between Tony and one of his brothers a week or two ago where he was seriously considering calling the whole wedding off because he wasn't in love with Bridget, just Alexis, and he wants her back."

It made me pissed that this guy was still hung up on my girl, even after everything he'd put her through. The bear inside me was twisting in rage, wanting to come out and find Tony.

"There's more bro. It...it doesn't look good, but you gotta know."

"What?" I asked.

"I hacked into Tony's texts on his phone and was scanning them. I found a message chain between Tony and Lex from about two days ago. They've planned a meet up tonight. They planned on doing it out of town so no one would see them together."

I took a stumbling step back from Rogue, not believing him.

"No man, you misread them. Maybe he has another girl on the side named Lex too."

"As unlikely as that is, I checked that too. I cross referenced the numbers. It's for sure Lex's phone he's communicating with."

Rage sent a red film across my vision, like my heart was breaking. Would she really fuck around on me? With that fucking tool? Or was that what all this was? Some way to get Tony jealous enough to finally call off the wedding and get back with her. Was I really a pawn in some fucked up rich girl game? But she'd never go back to him. She'd talked about it so much. She hated Tony, didn't she? If she did, why would she want a secret meeting with him tonight? Tonight of all nights? A night so important to Zachary.

Unbidden a flash filled my mind. Tony bending Lex over his car hood thrusting into her out in the woods somewhere. Her whimpering in pleasure. I gritted my teeth and squinted my eyes, shoving the image out of my mind.

"Rogue track her phone, tell me where she is."

He sighed. "I was sure you were going to ask that. Way ahead of you." He handed me a piece of paper with an address on it. "That's the last pinged location for her phone before I came up here.

I shoved the paper into my pocket and jogged over to Grizz. "Hey man. I got some shit going on, can you watch over Zachary for me?"

Grizz frowned. "What kind of shit? You need back up?"

I explained everything the Rogue had just told me.

Grizz put a hand on my shoulder. "Don't be rash Sting. I know Lex too. That doesn't sound like her. I'm sure it's something other than what you think it is."

I nodded and went to my bike. I really hoped Grizz was right. I wanted to believe it. I needed to.

Chapter 21 - Alexis

It took a lot of guts and multiple deleted texts before I worked up the courage to send the first text to Tony. Setting up the meeting was something I needed, and I wanted it over as soon as possible. My suspicions were already raised. After the first text he seemed to be crazy eager to see me. He was marrying my sister, he should not be eager to see me at all. Even then he agreed to meet up with me.

I'd considered telling Sting, but I didn't want to add more stress to his life. He had enough to worry about with his business and Zachary. I didn't want him to think I needed protection or something. This meeting was going to be a quick conversation, in and out. Then Tony would finally be out of my life for good.

Tony arrived right on time. I'd set the meeting for a few towns over. A solid forty minute drive from Forest Heights. I didn't need some nosey ass seeing us and spreading rumors. He looked nervous when he got out of his car.

"Hey," he said, walking toward me. "I have to say I'm a little surprised you wanted to see me. I'm so glad you did though."

"Stop right there. I want to make it clear, this is not some secret tryst. I'm not here to ask you to take me back okay?"

His shoulders visibly slumped and I cursed myself. That's exactly what he thought this was. It pissed me off to no end.

"You need to be ashamed of yourself. You're marrying Bridget but you don't love her at all? What the fuck Tony? You made me witness all this shit, made me go through all the crap Mom and Bridget put me through because of...what? Why?"

He opened his mouth several times to start, but couldn't find the words. He looked like a fish out of water gasping for breath.

Finally he slumped even more and said, "Okay, so. One night while we were in school Bridget came over looking for you. To the apartment right? You weren't there so we hung out talking, and...one thing led to another and we ended up having sex. I felt pretty shitty about it afterward, but Bridget held it over my head. She kept telling me that she'd tell you what happened if I didn't do what she wanted.

"Thankfully I wast drafted a couple months later, and I looked at it as an *out*. So, I took it. That did mean leaving you too. I swear I had every intention of getting back with you once Bridget's whole thing blew over. But after a few years, too much time had passed. Then I got injured and I was done with football.

"Bridget was kind of...there you know? It was weird because I honestly didn't like her that much."

I cut in. "You didn't like her? But you liked her enough to fuck her while we were dating, and then marry her after you retired?"

He nodded reluctantly. "It sounds bad when you say it like that but yeah, basically. She was just the thing I needed at the right time. It was...I just kind of fell into it. I honestly didn't realize we were in a serious relationship until she informed me that, oh yes, we were. After everything she'd done for me I didn't argue. It was like I was obligated, and now I'm stuck. It never felt right.

"Lex, I never stopped loving you. I never expected things with your sister to get this out of hand. It's like I'm trying to climb out of a sand pit but the sides keep caving in and I can't get out. But I don't care anymore. I'm calling the wedding off. It's over."

I shook my head, exasperated by everything he'd said, "If you do that then you need to do it for yourself and not in some attempt to get me back. That isn't happening. I don't love you any more. I don't even have any romantic thoughts about you. This won't change the way I feel."

Tony slumped and leaned onto his car. "I kind of thought you'd say that. I'd held out hope when you messaged me, but was sure it was a one in a million chance. You are right though, I'm ending it for me. Not for anyone else. I don't love Bridget, I love you. It isn't fair to anyone for me to go through with this when I feel like that. Once I tell her I'm going to move on with my life. I'll get out of Forest Heights, neither of you will have to see me again. Maybe I'll try to get into coaching or something."

I was actually sad for him. For the whole situation really, the fact that it came to this. But it was for the best.

My voice was gentler when I said, "I hope you do well Tony."

"Can I at least buy you dinner as a half assed apology for everything?"

I chewed my lip, wondering if there was an ulterior motive.

Tony seemed to see the thoughts on my face and raised his hands in surrender. "Seriously, just dinner. I want to catch up. I want...I want to know about you. You know, to make sure all my shit hasn't messed your life up too bad."

I laughed. "Tony, I think you have a big head. It's not that bad." I thought for a second before saying. "Well okay, it was pretty bad."

I stared at him without smiling for several seconds, letting him sweat. Then burst out laughing. His face broke into a grin, and he joined me laughing.

"Okay, yeah, I deserve that. So, for real can I get you something to eat?"

I rolled my eyes. "Fine, but nothing fancy. There's a burger joint over there, we can get something there."

"Fantastic."

Tony walked with me to the burger place, making sure to keep a respectable distance from me. It was nice that he wasn't trying to crowd me, or get cuddly or anything. I really believed that he was being sincere. It was too late for us to have anything, way too late. I still felt bad for him though. One bad mistake with my sister had pretty much ruined his life. You had to live with the consequences of your actions, but it didn't

mean people couldn't feel sorry for you.

We sat waiting for our food to come out,

and talked about random things at first. The

weather, my job, his football career. It took a bit

but he finally broached the subject I knew he

really wanted to talk about.

"So, how's this Sting guy treating you?"

"He's actually really great. I love him, like

really, really love him."

Tony looked at me and a smile spread

slowly across his face, and he nodded.

"I'm happy for you Lex."

I could see that he really wasn't, but at last

he was making an attempt. The server took our

order and brought our drinks out a few seconds later.

"Wait. I remember this." He pulled the little container of sweeteners toward him. "You like tea but with three supar packets and two Splenda packets right?"

I grinned. "Good memory."

He tore open all five packets and poured them into my tea.

"Thank you." I said.

The food came out later and we ate, mostly in silence. We did chit chat about a few things here and there, but it was a little awkward. It wasn't the goodbye I'd really wanted. If I was honest with myself, having dinner with him was mostly out of pity on my part. We finished and I was relieved when it was time to head back to my car.

"Can I walk you?" Tony asked.

I shrugged. "Okay, sure."

We started strolling to my car at the far end of the parking lot.

"So, I wanted to say thanks for meeting up with me. And giving me a chance to explain things and make you see why everything went down the way it did."

I was suddenly nauseous and dizzy, I was worried the burger I had wasn't agreeing with me. I made it to my car and put a hand on the hood to steady myself. What the fuck was wrong with me?

Tony sighed and put his hands in his pockets. "Well I guess this is goodbye...hey are you alright? You don't look so good. Lex?"

I put a hand to my face, covering my eyes. "Everything is spinning. I don't feel good, like I'm high or something."

"Well you shouldn't drive. Get in with me, and I'll take you to my place."

His place? Something didn't seem right. I felt like shit but even in this state I could tell something was off. Then my mind clicked back to the moment Tony put the sugars in my drink.

"Did...you...drug...me?" I could barely get the words out, I was already slumping against the car unable to stand.

Without a word Tony slid his arms under my armpits and started dragging me to his car. I tried kicking and fighting him, but it was like I was a baby. I couldn't even slap at him.

"Why did it have to take all this?" Tony asked, grunting as he pulled me along. "You don't understand how much I still love you. But you'll remember how good we are together. I needed to get you away from that white trash biker." He slid me in the passenger seat and buckled me. "After tonight it'll be like old times."

The last thing I remembered was Tony leaning forward and kissing me. I wanted to lash out, punch him, hit him, something. Instead I was locked inside my own mind, watching this terrible movie play out through my eyes. Then even those

slid closed.

Chapter 22 - Sting

I needed answers. It didn't make any sense, and I had to know what the hell was going on. I gassed my bike and rocketed down the highway toward the address Rogue had given me. As though he heard me think his name, my phone rang. The cell was locked in place by a phone cradle between my handle bars. I hit the green button and the bluetooth speaker in my ear beeped.

"Sting."

"Yeah what's up?"

"Something weird man. Lex's location is changing. She's moving fast, but not toward home."

For some reason this news put me even more on edge. "Stay on the phone while you track her."

A few seconds later I saw the diner where Lex was supposed to have been. Her car was still in the parking lot.

"Rogue, her car is still here? She hasn't gone anywhere."

"Uh...well maybe she...went with someone else?"

I growled and pulled into the parking lot. I got off the bike and checked her car. It was still locked, no one inside.

"Sting man, I've got three guys with me. We are already heading toward you for back up."

I gritted my teeth. Better safe than sorry. "Yeah sure. Get down here fast."

I walked to the diner and stepped inside. It was pretty empty, only a small family in the back, a young girl acting as server, she was maybe twenty-two or twenty-three, and a couple of cooks behind the line.

"Excuse me miss?" I said to the server.

"What can I do for you mister?"

"Did a young lady happen to be here a little while ago? Black hair, curly. Light brown skin, very attractive?"

"Yeah. She just left. I don't know, five minutes ago. Haven't even gotten their table cleared yet."

"She was with someone else?"

She nodded. "Big athletic fella, nice hair. Seemed kinda skeezy to me though. Kept looking at her like she was a piece of meat."

She stepped over to the table and grabbed the glasses to start clearing it. My stomach clenched in knots. Had she really come here with, and left with Tony?

The girl continued. "They left in the same car. She looked kinda out of it, though. Like she was drunk, but all she had was this...oh shit."

The girl turned back to me, gaping at her hand. I stared at her, confused.

"Mister, do you know that girl? Because I think she's in trouble."

"What are you talking about?" I asked, trying not to scream.

She held her hand out toward me. All of her nails were painted a bright neon blue. All except for the middle finger. That one was half blue half green. I stared at her hand, still confused. I was also getting angry. Could she not get to the damned point?

"What am I looking at?" I asked.

She sighed. "It's special nail polish. I put it on when I go out to a club or a bar. The polish is made to change color if you dip it into your drink as it's been drugged. Some guys tried making it a few years ago and couldn't. Some friends of mine at school are working on a version that does work. This is like ninety percent accurate." She exclaimed, pointing at her finger.

A growl worked its way out of my throat. Tony had drugged her? That piece of shit. My blood was boiling.

"Rogue, did you hear that?" I said, hoping the ear piece was still active.

"Uh, yeah. That's fucked up. We are almost there. I'll have the guys get Lex's car back and find the police."

"I'm calling the cops. Right now." The girl said, pulling her phone out of her apron.

"His name is Tony Givens," I said to her as I ran out the door.

"Rogue man, where is Lex? Are you still tracking her?"

"Yeah he's heading north on the interstate, take a right out of that parking lot, go three miles and take the northbound exit. He's got a head start but I'll update you if he gets off."

I jumped onto the bike and kicked it to life, peeling rubber as I pulled out of the parking lot.

The next forty-five minutes seemed like hours, days even. I wondered for a minute if Tony was going to try to take Lex to Canada.

"Sting?" Rogue said.

"Go."

"They've pulled off the interstate. Looks like exit three-forty-two. It's roughly thirty miles ahead of you. They went about three miles and now they've stopped. You better move brother."

I gassed the bike, letting the rpms redline. I didn't give a shit if I blew the engine as long as I made it to Lex before that son of a bitch touched her. My speedometer ticked past ninety, then a hundred. The wind screamed by me, I passed cars and semis like they were sitting still as I flew toward her. The fires of hell were behind me, pushing me on. The only thing I could think was that this might be the day I actually killed someone.

Thirty minutes later I finally pulled into the area Rogue had directed me to. It was a small farm town. A dinky little downtown area surrounded by dozens of massive farms. Each neighbor miles away from the other. I was beginning to panic. It had taken me a half hour from the time they stopped for me to get here. I didn't want to think of all the things Tony could have done to Lex in that amount of time. I parked my bike a good distance from the house, so Tony wouldn't hear me coming.

"Sting, we're right behind you. Be there in maybe fifteen or twenty minutes. I'm going to get off here. See you soon. Be careful man."

My feet whispered through the grass as I jogged to the house, as quietly as I could manage. The lights were on downstairs, and there was a shadow moving past one of the windows. I hunkered down by a window listening.

Lex's voice, groggy and faint, came to me through the window.

"Why are...you doing this?"

"Because I love you. I need to remind you that you love me too."

"Sting...he'll kill you...when he finds...out."

"Oh, he can try. I'm not scared of you furry little friend. You know what? Bears can go down with a bullet just the same as a man can."

Lex's voice got stronger. "I'd never forgive you. If you hurt him."

"What the fuck do you mean. Look at me. Look at him. He's a fucking mongrel, trailer trash, illiterate biker. Why in the name of god are you doing this? What the fucking hell is wrong with you?"

Sitting there listening to Lex defend me, I felt like shit. I should have never doubted her. It made me sick to think about all the scenarios I'd played in my head on the way to the diner. I had to push those thoughts away though. I couldn't sit here

full of self pity, when Lex was in trouble.

Tony said, "You know what? I know what the

problem is. You've forgotten how good we were

together. All those nights, alone. I can still

remember what your skin tastes like. I need to

show you what it was like and it will all come back

to you. A night with me and you'll forget all about

your little teddy bear."

His belt buckle snapped open, and Lex cried

out. I forgot about waiting for backup. I forgot

about staying safe. I forgot that he said he'd shoot

me. All I knew was I had to get in there. Right

then.

I sprinted to the front door and kicked it in. Inside on the couch Tony looked up in shock. He was on top of Lex, one hand trying to pull her shirt up, the other down at his pants working the zipper down.

"Sting." Lex's voice was the last thing I registered before the heat of rage muffled my hearing and I dove at Tony, roaring.

I can't remember the fight. Not even the first punch. It had to have gone on for a while. When I came too Rogue and Trey were pulling me off Tony. Blood was everywhere and my hands were covered in it. I was gasping for breath and dripping with sweat. Tony laid on the floor, still alive, groaning. Both eyes were swollen shut, his nose was broken, and it looked like he'd lost some teeth.

"Bro, Lex needs you man," Rogue said, pushing me toward her.

She was passed out on the couch again. Rushing to her, I took her in my arms and patted her cheek, trying to wake her up. Rogue was on the phone to 911, but the only thing I was concerned with was Lex.

Her eyes fluttered open. "He...drugged me again...just...before we...got here."

Again? Had he overdosed her by accident? I looked over at the beaten and bloody man on the floor and wanted to get up and kick his ass all over again. Instead I looked at Rogue.

"Rogue, she needs help. She might be overdosing on whatever he gave her."

"They're like five minutes out. The girl at the diner called earlier and I called them again once I was sure of the address. Any minute now."

Almost like magic, the sound of sirens filled my ears as he finished. Glancing up the electric blue of police lights, and the red and white lights of an ambulance filled the dark sky. I breathed a sigh of relief as the EMT rushed in and immediately went to work. One on Tony, the other on Lex. The EMT confirmed she was more than likely overdosed, and started her on an IV to flush her system.

The ride in the back of the ambulance with her was the scariest time of my life. I could have lost her. Could still lose her. The monitors beeped and the sirens hurt my sensitive ears. My heart raced with worry as the paramedics did all they could. If she'd been a shifter she would've been protected. She would've healed, metabolized it off.

I tried to stay pressed out of the way with one hand on Alexis anywhere I could reach. All I could think of was that if we got out of this ok, I would never let her out of my sight again.

Chapter 23 - Alexis

The first sound that broke through the silence was a quiet beeping. It took a while but I finally opened my eyes and saw I was in a hospital bed. My head was going to explode. What happened? Why was I here? I looked down and saw wires attached to me, and tubes running into me. A wave of panic overcame me.

The memories of the night before trickled into my mind. Anxiety flooded me. I breathed fast, almost hyperventilating. The thought about what had happened was almost too much to process. Then there was a hand, soft and cool on my arm.

"Babe, you're okay." Sting was there.

I had a faint memory of Sting beating the shit out of Tony, before everything went black.

My voice sounded like I hadn't spoken in weeks when I asked, "Did you kill him?"

Sting froze for a moment, his face set. "Would you be upset if I did?"

I sighed and sank into the pillow. "I'm in a hospital bed hooked up to all kinds of shit because of Tony. Do I want him dead? No. If only for the fact that you'd probably go to jail."

Sting ran a hand across his face. "I'm sorry." He shook his head and changed the subject, "I was so worried about you. Are you okay?"

"My head's like it's in a vice, but other than that I'm okay. How the hell did you find me anyway?" I asked. The question nagging at me.

He froze, and chewed his lip. He looked like someone who had something to say, but was something they really didn't want to say.

"Just spit it out Sting."

He winced and said, "I had Rogue dig into Tony's stuff. It was right after he came and accosted me at the lounge. He hacked his phone, just to check his search history, texts, GPS location. Stuff like that. He...ended up getting into your phone too...that's...that's how I knew you were at the diner with him. And how you ended up at the house out there."

A strange combination of love, irritation, rage, shock, and happiness flooded me. I wanted to slap the shit out of him, kiss him, and berate him all at the same time. I was pissed at him, but grateful too. How the hell do I get mad at him for not trusting me when, by not trusting me, he saved me from getting raped and probably worse?

It didn't stop me from unloading on him a bit. "You realize you can't go around lojacking your girlfriend because you're insecure or whatever? It's not how healthy relationships start Sting."

"Grade-A dumbass, got it. You were being secretive. You didn't give me a good reason to not come to the pack meet. Then when Rogue found those texts between you and Tony...I thought the worst. Which was stupid. I should have called or texted you and gotten the real story. I know I don't have anything to worry about, I'm really just happy you're safe."

Before I could respond, the door opened and a doctor walked in.

"Miss King?"

"Yes?"

"I'm Doctor Jones, I wanted to check in. Give you an update on treatment."

"Sure, what did it take? Am I on the mend?"

He shrugged and flipped through the chart. "I'd love to say it was a strange case, but unfortunately we have a lot of experience with overdoses. You'd ingested it more than an hour before we got to you so activated charcoal or an emetic wouldn't work. We got a bunch of fluids into you to help flush the body and a dose of Flumazenil. It's a benzodiazepine antidote, since it was Rohypnol you'd been dosed with it worked well."

"He roofied me."

"Seems that way. I've dealt with it a lot in college towns. Men can be garbage, if you forgive my bluntness."

I fell back into the pillows. "No. That's entirely accurate."

The Doctor continued. "Just so you know. Mister Givens is being treated here. He'll be here for several days but will then be released to the police. It was extensive. Nose broken in two places, two cracked orbital bones, broken jaw, black eyes, three cracked teeth, two missing teeth, three broken ribs, and multiple." He glanced at Sting approvingly. "*Multiple* contusions. I have daughters myself, young man. Don't tell anyone I said this, I would get in trouble, but, good job son."

I glanced at Sting who looked at the floor embarrassed. He shrugged and stayed silent.

The doctor said, "Your vitals are all good. I want one more bag of fluid to go through you, and I think you'll be good to go through discharge. Let me know if you have any questions."

As the doctor left Sting said, "Umm, so... I guess I should let you know. I called your family so they know what went down."

I sat up, my head immediately spinning from the quick movement. "What?"

Before Sting could explain more the door to the room opened and my mom, Dad and sister piled in. It was like they'd rehearsed it. Goose flesh burst out on my arms and legs. My fight or flight sense went into overdrive. I didn't know how I would handle Mom and Bridget. Not in this state. I hoped Dad would hold them in check. Before anyone could speak, Sting stepped in front of my bed.

"I will toss every one of you out on your ass if you think about stressing her out. That is a promise."

I could see Bridget was seething, almost beyond comprehension, She fully ignored Sting's threat and started in on me.

"Lex what the fuck? You screwed every damn thing up. All this was your fault. Why couldn't you leave me and Tony alone. Now our wedding is ruined. And this fucking *beast* almost killed him. Tell her Mom. Tell her what an ungrateful bitch she is."

I glanced, fearfully at Mom, and was shocked to see her with tears in her eyes. Her lower lip quivering as she looked at me. Bridget looked as confused as I felt. I became even more befuddled when Mom ran forward. Arms outstretched.

"My baby...oh god. My baby." She enveloped me in a hug.

I couldn't remember the last time she'd hugged me like this. It wasn't the quick pat she would give someone at a cocktail party, or the side hug I might get during a family picture. It was the hug of a mother, holding a child she loved. I was stunned into silence.

Still holding me, Mom said, "I never thought I would get a call that one of my kids was in the hospital. My first thought was that you were...gone. When I thought that? Everything I'd ever said to you flashed across my mind. I'd

always thought I was trying to make you into the

girl I wanted you to be. I saw that I'd only made

you sad and miserable and...I would have had to

live with that guilt the rest of my life."

I sighed, It was nice. Though it also sounded

like it was more about Mom trying to appease her

own guilt rather than truly worrying about me.

But it was a start. It was more than she'd given in

years and years. I would accept it gratefully. I

wouldn't push. One step at a time.

Bridget was staring at Mom like she'd grown a

second and third head.

"What the fuck mom? You don't think Tony

did this do you? She fucking drugged her self and

sicked her pet bear on Tony. All to ruin my wedding. *My* special day. She couldn't handle the fact that Tony loves me now and she tried to ruin everything."

Dad stepped forward, opening his mouth to shut her up, but I beat him to the punch. "Listen Bridget. Your *fiance*? Doesn't love you. He fucked you to get close to me. When he tried to pour his feelings out and I told him he had no chance? He drugged me. He kidnapped me, and was seconds away form raping me if Sting hadn't showed up."

Mom and Dad's faces went slack with horror and shock. Bridget's face was blood red and she was shaking her head like a child who wasn't getting their way.

"No. Not true. Tony told me everything...well...he wrote everything. He can't talk because his jaw is wired shut thanks to that asshole." She waved a dismissive hand at Sting. "He said you lured him out to that farmhouse and let Sting beat the shit out of him in a jealous rage. That is exactly what happened."

I shook my head at how oblivious she was. Oblivious or desperate, not wanting to believe what is right in front of her face.

"I'm sticking with Tony. It'll be us against you. Right Daddy?" She turned a hopeful look on Dad.

His face was clouded with anger. "If you want to be with the man who tried to molest my daughter. The man who kidnapped her and put her life at risk? Then you are on your own sweet heart. I will love you forever, but I'll have nothing to do with that piece of shit."

Bridget looked like she'd been slapped. Her face crumpled into tears.

She stomped out, calling behind her as the door closed. "I never get anything. This is such bullshit."

I put my hand on mom's. "You believe me right, Mom?"

Dad was nodding, looking sad. Mom whispered sadly. "Yes, baby. I do. And I'm so sorry."

I was released about three hours later, Sting drove us home in his truck.

Glancing toward me he said, "Zachary is still staying with Grizz and Zoey. He'll be there until you have your strength back, and you're ready to meet him."

I couldn't wait to meet him. I'd heard so much about the kid, but I was more tired than I'd ever been in my life, so I nodded and laid my head back napping on the way home. Sting carried me up to bed and got in, cuddling with me. It didn't seem like he wanted to let me go.

"Sting, are you okay?"

His body shivered. "I was so scared of losing you. Just watching the guys in the ambulance and the hospital work on you? And before that? I thought I was going to be too late and Tony might have done something to you. I've never in my life been so murderous. So helpless. You mean so much to me. So much. I think I'd die without you."

A lump formed in my throat and I put a hand to my chest. I'd never been so touched by anything someone had said. It was all the more emotional for me, because I felt the same about him.

Chapter 24 - Sting

My Mom stopped by the next morning. She'd heard about everything, and wanted to check in on us and make sure Lex was okay. She entered, trying to be quiet, and gave me a hug.

"How is the poor dear?"

I sat down heavily and said, "She's going to be good. Mom, can I talk to you about something?"

"Of course. You know I'm here for you. What's wrong?"

I sighed, tried to think of how to explain it and said, "Should I really be with her?"

Mom looked confused. "Lex? Don't you love her?"

"I do. That's the problem. I'm...so scared of what's going on inside me. Mom...I don't know what to do with these feelings. Everything is so damned intense. I keep wondering if it's worth it. Is it? Worth it I mean?"

Mom said, "I understand how hard it is. You've never been in love before. There are so many things that are scary about that, scary and intimidating, and...wonderful. You have to think about everything you have to gain by embracing the fear. Let your heart have what it wants. That is almost always a great way to have a fulfilling life."

My heart was lighter after listening to her. I nodded, knowing as usual, she was right.

"Now let me get a look at your kitchen. I'm going to cook you all a nice big family dinner, and you being a bachelor, I'm sure I'll need to make a grocery run to get what I need. Probably nothing but bologna and cheese in this place."

Mom had taken the news about Zachary well. She'd become attached to the kid quickly because, in her words, 'He was just like Sting when he was that age'. She wanted to be there when Lex and Zachary finally met. As support for me *and* Lex. An extra familiar face might make things a little easier on the kid meeting yet another new person.

While rummaging in the pantry Mom said, "Back to the other discussion. Are you ready to leave the playboy life behind? Do you want Zachary to grow up with that as an example? More things to consider."

I smiled. "The answers are no and no."

She walked over and patted me on the cheek. "Good boy. Then you know what needs to be done." She kissed me on the forehead. "I'll be back with food and get started."

"Thanks for always being there for me Mom."

As she closed the door behind her she said, "That's what moms are for."

That night Grizz brought Zachary over to finally meet Lex. I had to admit, it went better than I thought. Lex had been nervous until the boy walked in and locked eyes on her. His mouth dropped open

Zachary said, "You're…like…*waaaaay* prettier than I thought you'd be."

Everyone laughed, and I said, "Hey, bud, she's spoken for. You'll need to find your own when you get older." Dinner went well other than Zachary hanging around Lex the entire night. She was so gentle and calm with him by the end of the night you would have never known they'd only meet that day.

A few days later I called Kim. I'd made my decision, and I needed help. I explained what I wanted to do, and Kim took charge. She formulated a plan and assisted me with my grand idea. It didn't really take alot, just a bunch of hope that Lex would go along with it all.

Kim texted a few days after our initial discussion letting me know that she was taking Lex out for a girls night and they were coming to the lounge like we planned. Lex didn't know that I'd booked the club for a private party. It would just be me and her.

"Oh great. When will you guys get there?" I asked.

"I told her I'd pick her up around six. So, be ready for us by six-thirty."

"Will do."

I hung up and butterflies took over my stomach. Hope. That was what I felt deep inside. I prayed that it wasn't misplaced. She loved me too, right? This had to work.

Kim and Lex arrived and as they walked in the door Lex's face slackened in surprise. I'd scattered rose petals all over the floor leading from the door right to me and a table with two glasses and champagne. There was music playing overhead, and not another soul was in the place. Kim ducked back out the door as Lex started walking toward me.

"What is all this?" she asked.

I stepped forward and took her by the hand.

"I'm claiming what's mine."

"Look Sting, before you say whatever you're
going to say, I have to tell you something. I really
was going to tell you about the meeting with Tony
once it was all over. I never, ever had any
intentions of hiding anything from you. I know
how protective you are and thought you might
give me hell about wanting to get some kind of
closure with him."

I smiled wryly. "I can't argue with that. You
already know me well. I'm sorry I overreacted
before too. I never should have made you think I

didn't want to be with you. I hope all this can be put behind us?"

She nodded and smiled. My heart lifted.

"I love you Alexis King. More than anything I've ever loved in my life. I can't go another day without letting you know how deep my feelings go. The very thought of that asshole touching you drove me insane. I...what's wrong?"

She'd gone rigid while I spoke. She had a funny smile on her face, and said, "Repeat that again?"

My brow furrowed as I thought. It took a second to realize what she was talking about. I laughed.

"Well dammit It's true. I love you. I meant it and I mean everything else I'm about to say. I want you to be my mate. I will always talk to you and treat you as an equal. I will not lash out in anger, and I want us to talk things out and not jump to conclusions. I want to claim you in every way possible. I want to have babies with you. Even if you aren't able to carry my cubs, and Zachary is the only kid we get to raise then so be it. At least it will be with you. That would make me the happiest I've ever been. I want you in my life to love until the day we die. So, what do you say? Will you have me?"

She was crying tears of happiness as I finished talking. She answered by pulling me to her and kissing me. I could taste her tears as we kissed. She pulled away and put her forehead on my chest.

"I want all those same things. Everything you want, I want. And I want it right now."

She looked up at me, fire in her eyes. I could smell her arousal, and the bear clawed at me to make the move we both wanted. I scooped her up and kissed her as I carried her up the stairs to the apartment I kept above the lounge.

I laid her gently on the bed and covered her face, and neck in kisses as she worked my belt free and unzipped my pants. The cool smoothness of her fingers slid down and encircled me. I moaned and looked into her eyes. I stood and pulled my clothes off frantically. I ripped my white

dress shirt off, spraying buttons across the room.

Lex laughed. And I helped her pull her own clothes

off.

Finally free I pressed my naked body into hers,

letting her warmth seep into me. Her nipples were

hard and slid across my chest. I lowered my head

and took one in my mouth sucking at it, flicking

my tongue across the puckered flesh. Lex groaned

as I teased her with my mouth, running her fingers

through my hair. I cupped her cheek with one

hand and slid a finger inside her with the other,

loving the look of delighted surprise on her face. I

slid my tongue as I moved my finger in and out of

her, faster and faster, until her hips were jerking against my hand.

She lifted my head and looked me in the eyes,and whispered, "I need more than a finger."

"What about this?"

I lowered my face, my head pointing toward her feet and buried my tongue inside her, sliding my lips across her clit as I worked at her.

"Fuck." She groaned.

She took my cock in her mouth then, working at me with her mouth, as I worked at her with mine. Seconds of pleasure expanded into an eternity of passion. Her mouth was like heaven, wet, warm, hungry. I was getting close. Not wanting to finish yet, I pulled away from her and slid between her legs and looked into her eyes.

She whispered, "Come on big boy. Show me what you've got."

I grinned and slid into her, achingly slow. Inch by inch, watching her expression. Open mouthed ecstasy as I filled her. Finally inside her I clutched her breasts and gently played with her nipples as I began thrusting into her. Lex's hands reached behind me, clutching my ass, forcing me to move faster. Her hips rising and falling to meet me, matching my rhythm. In moments we were slamming into each other, bringing one another ever closer to the edge. The entire time our eyes locked onto each other, sharing the moment in the most intimate way possible.

"I'm close. Claim me Sting. Do it. I want it."

The words set off an explosion in my mind. The bear leapt to the fore, it was all I could do to keep myself in control and hold him at bay. I rolled Lex over and buried my cock in her again from behind. Three fast and deep thrusts and she began to scream my name as she came. My own climax was seconds away. When it happened, it was like a grenade going off in my loins, and I bit into the spot between her shoulder blades, claiming her forever as my mate as I came. Collapsing against her and pulling her into my arms a moment later. I was more content and happy than ever in my life. She reached a hand up and caressed my face as we fell asleep.

We slept late and headed over to Grizz's to tell them the good news and pick up Zachary. Grizz and Zoey were ecstatic and demanded we stay for a barbeque. Zachary was still hanging around Lex, asking her questions like crazy. And like before Lex was patient with him. Giving him the love and time a mother would. A mother Zachary was desperate for after losing his. It filled my heart to bursting watching them together.

I was outside on the deck helping Grizz grill when he patted my shoulder and said, "I know you guys had a little drama, but at least it wasn't as bad as what me and Hutch went through."

I laughed. "Well maybe Rogue was right when he said we should avoid human women."

"Well, I wouldn't have it any other way," Grizz said.

I looked through the window and watched Lex and Zachary playing a board game with Rainer and Zoey.

I grinned like a happy idiot. "Yeah, me either."

Chapter 25 - Rogue

Valentine's day was like a week and half away, and it was Misty's birthday. I was supposed to be meeting the new dude she'd been dating, it was weird. She'd never asked me to meet one of her guys before. I guess she'd never been serious enough about any of them for me to get introduced. Honestly I never gave her dating life much thought.

I parked my bike outside Sting's Lounge, not daring to let one of his valet's park my baby. The party started about fifteen minutes earlier, but it shouldn't be a big deal. I was wrong of course.

"Rogue. You're late. What the hell?" Lex called me out as soon as I stepped through the doors.

She'd gotten pretty feisty since getting with Sting, some of him was rubbing off on her. She even flipped me off. It made us both laugh.

"Sorry, I know. I'm here now though. Where's the birthday girl anyway?"

Lex pointed over to the corner. Misty was with a few friends and had some guy draped all over her. I felt my bear shift uneasily at the sight of it. I pushed the emotions aside, not sure where they came from. Instead walking over to her.

She glared at me and said, "You're late."

She stood and gave me a hug looking a little disheartened. "Rogue, you could at least have showered before coming."

I realized with a wince that I probably still smelled like the late afternoon hookup I'd had at the clubhouse before heading over. I rubbed my neck and felt something on it. Pulling my hand back, I pressed my lips together. Lipstick.

Misty gave me a sad look. She looked a little hurt and disappointed in me. It made me look like a dick. I am a dick. Self proclaimed, but never to Misty.

"Sorry, kind of a shit thing to do."

She shook her head. "It doesn't matter. At least you showed up." Her voice was listless and sad. It made my heart hurt.

Her smile returned when she gestured toward the guy she was with. "This is Harlem."

To me? He looked like an uptight dickwad, but I had to keep that to myself.

I extended a hand. "Rogue, good to meet you."

He leaned forward lazily and took my hand, but not firmly. Barely even squeezing it before letting go.

"What kinda name is that?" he asked.

I bit back a retort. Whe the fuck was he to make fun of my nick name when he was called fucking *Harlem?* Something about the guy didn't sit right with me but I laughed at his joke and acted like it didn't bother me.

The whole night my feelings about the guy grew steadily worse. He was never more than an arm's length away from Misty, always keeping a hand on her. It seemed possessive in all the wrong ways. He was even telling her which and how many drinks she could have. How the hell was he to tell what to drink on her damned birthday?

Misty tried to ask the bartender for a Long Island Iced Tea and Harlem cut her off. "Babe, nah. Just get a beer or something. You don't need that."

I'd had enough. "Hey Brooklyn or Bronx or whatever your name is, let the lady get what the hell she wants. It's her freaking special day alright."

"Rogue it's fine, don't worry about it," Misty said, even though it was clear it wasn't.

Harlem didn't seem to like that and stepped up until his chest met mine. Classic bar cock behavior.

"Hey my man. You need to back the fuck off. This is my woman. You don't have a say about shit."

My bear, to say the least, did not like that. I growled low and fierce. Everyone at the lounge went silent and started watching us. Sting slid up to me out of nowhere, putting a hand on my shoulder.

"Rogue man, let's chill out a bit okay?" he said.

I didn't want to chill. I was coming out of my skin, for maybe the first time in my life. But I bit down and pushed the bear back down.

I glanced over at Misty. "Sorry for causing a scene. You didn't deserve this. Happy birthday. I'll see you later."

I pushed past Harlem and was out the door a few seconds later, pissed.

"Rogue."

I turned and saw Misty chasing after me.

"Misty, I said I'm sorry. Go back to your party and have fun."

"Why did you act like that in there?" she asked.

I sighed. "I don't know. I didn't like how that guy was treating you like property. He was managing you and bossing you around. It didn't seem healthy and it pissed me off."

Misty sighed. "That's just the way he is."

Frowning, I asked, "Are you okay with that?"

"Well he's nice to me and treats me well."

"And?"

"And what?"

I chuffed out a laugh. "Is that like, the bare minimum you require from a guy?"

I didn't mean to sound like a dick, but once the words were out of my mouth I knew that was exactly what I sounded like. I could see the hurt on her face too. I felt like shit.

"Hey, Misty, I didn't mean it like that. I'm sorry. I thought you wanted more for yourself than a guy like that."

She looked at me with a weird expression, then said, "I did want more. I wanted someone better. But they didn't want me."

My eyes went wide. "Well that dude is one big fucking loser, and an idiot."

She laughed and let me pull her into a hug, I said, "I only act the way I do because you're my best friend. I want what's best for you."

She hugged me tight. "I know that."

She looked up at me, and when we locked eyes, there was a massive ache in my chest. My bear clawed to get out and it all almost took my breath away.

"You...uh... should get back in there. It's your party right?"

She lifted a hand and cupped my cheek, her fingers cool and soft, almost making me gasp.

"Are you sure you're okay Rogue?"

I mimicked her movement and put a hand on her cheek, her skin velvety soft. "I am fine. I won't leave. I'll chill out here for a bit and come back inside later."

Nodding, she headed back into the lounge. I sat on the curb and a few minutes later Sting came outside. He walked toward me with a concerned look on his face.

"Hey man, Misty said she was worried about you."

I looked at him as he sat down beside me. I had a question I needed to ask, but was terrified to actually voice it. Putting things out into the world could have consequences. But I decided I needed an answer.

"Sting…how did you know Lex was the *one*?"

"Why are you asking?" The look on Sting's face told me he already had an idea.

"Would you stop dicking around with me? Just answer the question."

Laughing Sting asked, "One question. How does your bear react when she's around?"

"I feel the rumble in my chest. My possessive mood comes out. That couldn't be it though. It was because Misty is my friend. I care about her, so my bear must care too. She's like family."

Sting stared at me like I was an idiot.

I groaned, knowing it was more than that. Deep down I think it had always been more. I just didn't want to deal with it. It looked like my bear wasn't going to have any more waiting. It was pissed because someone else was creeping in on what was meant for them. Now that I knew the truth I couldn't allow that to happen now... could I?

Made in the USA
Monee, IL
01 September 2023

41974892R00270